"Go back to your own room!"

One of Gile's shoes clumped as it landed on the floor. "Think, Rose. We've got three bedrooms. Josie has one, the police inspector has one, and that leaves the last to be shared by us."

Rose could feel the panic rising within her. "What kind of logic is that?"

"Just shut up and move over, Rose. Mr. and Mrs. Gendron will spend a quiet night in the connubial nest, and the inspector will go back to Tahiti without a suspicion in the world."

The bed sank as he stretched out beside her. "I told you before I didn't want you to lay a hand on me."

"For heaven's sake," he muttered in her ear. "Close your eyes, and let's see if at least one of us can get some sleep before morning."

EMMA GOLDRICK

daughter of the sea

Harlequin Books

TORONTO • NEW YORK • LONDON
AMSTERDAM • PARIS • SYDNEY • HAMBURG
STOCKHOLM • ATHENS • TOKYO • MILAN

Harlequin Presents first edition March 1986
ISBN 0-373-10866-4

Original hardcover edition published in 1985
by Mills & Boon Limited

CHAPTER ONE

SHE struggled to open her right eye. The other was swollen shut. A vague male figure stood by the bed. She blinked, trying to bring it into focus.

'*Iorana oe*,' he said in a deep soothing baritone. The Polynesian words flowed melodically. She tried to repeat them, forming them deep in her parched throat, in the way he had sounded them 'Yorahna ohe?' He chuckled.

'What does that mean,' she croaked. He came closer to the bedside.

'*Iorana oe*,' he repeated. 'It means hello, goodbye, greetings.'

'Oh,' she sighed, disappointed.

'It also means *live happily*,' he added with another chuckle.

'Ever after?' she pleaded.

'Yes, if you like,' he said sympathetically. 'Live happily ever after.'

Her body stopped shivering for just a moment, and a feeling of peace welled over her. But her eyelid was too heavy. It blinked, closed, and she fell down into the maw of terror again.

The great waves which pounded and rolled the tiny rubber raft bounced her up and down, smashing her into the tiny case of stores in the bow until she was bruised and battered. Until she gave up the unequal fight, and withdrew into herself, coiling up in a foetal ball and letting the ocean do its will. At first she cried, clutched herself there in the darkness. She could see nothing. As she stepped aboard the little craft, her father had struggled to set up the tiny tent-like roof that kept the raft from foundering under the hammer blows of wind and rain. And then the deck had dipped under water, and the raft had floated free. She was still able to think, back then. She struggled to raise one corner of the tent and scream into the wind. But her father could not hear. It was the money again. He had pushed her into the life raft and had gone back into the cabin for the briefcase that held the money. And then he and the yacht had swung in one direction, the raft in the other, and the wild typhoon had blotted out the world.

She was too good a sailor to believe that it was the end for both of them. They had come too close to the rocky shore of Moorea, and the yacht had bounced off the rocks at Itihau Point. So that gave them two ways to drift. Around the point itself, under the pressure of the wind, and on to the little beaches of Itihau. Or out into the equatorial current, and up the chain of islands to wherever wind and sea would take them.

All that was in the first night, as wind and current battled for the tiny inflatable raft. She had laughed and cried and prayed and sang until her body had no strength to do more. And then she had withdrawn into the hidden corners of her mind, where no storms could follow. So she knew nothing, actually, of the next day, or the one that followed, when the great winds blew themselves out. And, as a sort of after-thought, tossed the little craft so high that it cleared the reef at Te Tuahine.

Gentler winds propelled the little orange raft across the lagoon and beached on the black sand just under the eastern point, where Mona Atau stood guard over the entrance to Pakua Bay.

It might have rested undiscovered into the heat of the tropical sun, if Sam Apuka had not drunk too much beer at the festival. Not *kaava*, the local fermented coconut drink, but imported beer, carried all the way from Tahiti in bottle. Although the *kaava*, on top of all that beer, might have been a factor. In any event, just before sunrise, Sam rolled off his sleeping mat, wandered out into the moonlight, and took care of his problem.

The moonlight was the trap. At forty, Sam Apuka knew the value of moonlight, the lure of hip-swinging *vahine*, the sound of the slack-string guitar. He kicked his toes in the sand and wandered up the beach, wondering if his head would ever stop pounding.

The orange brillance caught his attention. Eagerly he turned his attention to it. A new phenomenon in this tiny island world always drew a crowd. Sam knew what it was. After all, had he not worked for five years for CEP, the *Centre d'Experimentations du Pacifique?* That was before he caught *fiu*, of course.

It took only a minute for his gnarled hands to unfasten the ropes and throw back the cover. And by that time he had gathered a crowd. Two other men, pale bronze shadows in the moonlight, peering over his shoulder.

'What you got there, Sam?' one of them asked in the delightful mixture of French, Polynesian, and English that served this last island outpost of French Polynesia. '*Aue*, look at that. That some beautiful *vahine*, believe me, brother!' The three of them stared down at the contents of the rubber raft. One magnificently lovely girl, her long blonde hair hanging in wet strings around her oval face. She was curled up in the foetal position, knees up against her capacious breasts, hands wrapped around her legs. She might be five-foot-four, perhaps. Her eyes were closed, and dried salt cemented her eyelids together. She hardly appeared to be breathing. She wore a bright orange lifejacket strapped loosely around her torso, and nothing else.

'Man, that some *vahine* you got there!'

'I ain't got her,' Sam Apuka told him sternly. There was a need to speak sharply to the young men. The old ways were almost gone. The young grew up with no reverence. 'And she no *vahine*. Look at that hair. *Mon Dieu!* That one a *popa'a*—a European. *Te Tamahine Tanqora.* Daughter of the Sea, that who she is. Come on, you two. We carry her up to the Big House.'

She woke for the second time. The room was plain but cheerful. Bamboo framed it, and pandasu leaves, woven in strips, shielded the walls. There was a gap at the bottom and top of each wall, to let the breeze blow through. Sunlight was flashing at her. Three huge bamboo chairs barely cluttered the room. She was lying in a bed. Wide, comfortable—also of bamboo. Her hair clustered around her face, fresh-washed, smelling of coconut oil. But her lips were dry, thickened by salt rime, and her throat was parched.

'Now I sit up and look around,' she mumbled to herself, 'and somebody comes in and I say "Where am I," and he says, "Are you Rose Lambert?" And I say, "Yes, I'm Rose," and he says "Where's your Papa, Rose Lambert? We know all about both of you. And if we can't get him we've got you. I arrest you for embezzlement, woman." And I say—holy murder, I can't say any of that!'

There was a stirring at the side of the bed. She turned her head. A little girl nestled in one of the big bamboo chairs. Eight years old, perhaps—nine? Her adult teeth crowded her tiny mouth. Straight golden hair, knitted up into two pigtails, a gingham dress sat lightly on her shoulders, and fell to about mid-thigh. Obviously too small for her. She looked like a little elf who had been too long in some man's care.

Not a native girl. Not hardly. A peaches-and-cream complexion, highlighted by a line of tiny freckles that ran across one cheek, up the bridge of her nose, and out on to the other.

'Hello.' The child was cuddling a teddy bear, almost bigger than she. Well-scuffed, with one eye missing.

'Hello?'

'You been sleeping for a long time, did you know? It's the day after tomorrow already.'

'The day after tomorrow?'

'Well, the day before yesterday was the day you came, and then yesterday, and now is the day after, and all you've done is sleep.' Was there some accusation there? Rose struggled to clear the cobwebs. Obviously conversation was a desperate thing in this household! It might be better to go on the offensive.

'I like to sleep,' she said firmly. The little girl thought it over carefully.

'My name's Josie,' she contributed.

And there I am, caught in a dilemna, she told herself. Even with a child I can't make conversation. Make up a name? And then forget it the first chance, and put my foot in the soup? I need something simple!

'My name's Josie,' the child repeated, just a little bit louder. 'You haven't got deaf, have you?'

'No, I'm not deaf. That's a nice name. Does it stand for Josephina?'

'No, it just stands for Josie. I ain't supposed to ask you what your name is.'

'Oh? Did someone tell you that?'

'Yup. Daddy says it's supposed to be some kind of test. What is your name?'

'Josie, I hope you won't be angry with me—but I just don't remember.' And that's it, she told herself. The simplest form of lie. Don't ask me any questions, because I don't remember *anything*. No selective memories that can trip me up. I'll go all that way. Amnesia, isn't that what people get when they've been in shock? That's me. Forty-eight hours in a life raft, and I've got amnesia. And that's a story I can stick to through hell and high water!

'You don't remember your own name! Daddy, did you hear that?'

'Hear what, love?' He had come in so quietly she would not have known he was there, had not his daughter looked up. She must be his daughter. I wonder where his wife can be!

'I said my name was Josie and she said she can't remember *her* name. Ain't that funny?'

'Isn't, baby—not ain't. And no, it isn't funny. Didn't we say something about that?'

'You mean about I shouldn't ask? Well, I——'

'Hey, no additional dialogue, pest. Scoot out of here. Out!'

'But Daddy! She's a girl, and I ain't seen no girl this——'

'Not right now, pet. Our—lady is just recovering. Scoot.'

'Okay, meany. Shall I tell Miri to bring the meal?'

Rose watched the pair of them as they jousted. There was a deep affection there, betrayed by the look in their eyes, by the casual touching that spoke myriad messages, by the tilt of their heads as they talked. Two people who loved each other. Just the way Papa and I love each other!

The little girl is a beauty, and will grow into something more, Rose thought. The man—well, he's not exactly ugly, but he's far from handsome. There's a deep scar on his neck, behind his ear. And furrows down each side of his face. 'Worry lines,' her mother called them. His ears were rather small for such a large head, and his chin sported a vertical cleft of note. Brown hair, brown eyes. No, not handsome, but still rather—imposing? It was hard to read his expression. A man who kept his own secrets. He smiled at her.

'Do you want to get up?'

'I—I can't. I don't have any clothes.' And neither does he! He's wearing tight blue shorts, frayed at the legs, barely enough to cover the law. What law? A woman had come into the room. A Polynesian, carrying a jug of some liquid. She looked to be in her early twenties. She wore a brilliant red and yellow *pareau* draped around her hips. It fell to just above her ankles. And all the delightfully female rest of her was left on view!

'We can get you a *pareau*,' he continued. 'Like the one Miri is wearing. One size fits all.' There seemed to be a bubble of laughter in his voice. At least Rose chose to interpret it that way.

'If that's what she's wearing, I need considerably more than that,' she sighed. 'I don't seem to remember what I normally wear, but I'm sure it's more than that!'

'You don't remember anything at all?' That's what is sparking his interest, she noted. He's got that hawk-look on his face. There's something about my fake amnesia that interests him tremendously. What *is* it?

'No,' she returned vaguely. 'Nothing at all.' And as she watched him from under the fringe of her long eyelashes she would have sworn that he was relieved to hear it. He came over to the bed.

'Drink this.' He offered a glass of something cool. 'As soon as we restore your body fluids you'll feel better. There doesn't seem to be anything broken, although you have a number of bruises.'

She sipped eagerly at the glass. Orange juice. And something else, something unknown to her. 'Papaya juice,' he chuckled. There was a crackle of noise from some other room in the house. A radio!

'I have to run,' he said, and did. The girl called Miri came over and chattered at her in an odd mixture of Polynesian, French, and English. They wanted her out of the bed. She managed to fade their words into the background, and concentrate. The voice on the radio was speaking rapid-fire French, somewhat beyond her Louisiana *patois*. But she caught the gist of it. It was a call from the police on Tahiti, being relayed through the adjacent island of Maupiti. In the middle of the next sentence somebody turned something down, or closed a door, for the rest of the conversation was lost.

Oh God, she thought. The storm has gone, and it's clean-up time. Where is Jules François Lambert, who stole from the Banque Pacifique? Or his missing daughter, Rose. Where! The police would appreciate information in order to make an arrest. Oh God!

Supporting hands helped her to her feet. She forced her muscles to move her, across the room, where the little girl brushed the curtains aside, out into a long cool corridor angled so that the trade winds blew eternally down its length, and down three doors to the bathroom. It's what I do most every day, she told herself hysterically. Walk naked down the hall, held up by a tiny girl in a too-short dress, and a lovely *vahine* wearing next to nothing!

The bathroom was more than she expected. A tin shower-stall, open to the sky for one thing, and a complicated chain affair attached to a huge barrel poised overhead. A rather large enamel hand basin, with a plastic pipe coming out its bottom, and no taps. Of course, she sighed. All the water has to be carried. And then, the height of luxury, a Scandinavian chemical toilet! Not bad, considering.

Her two escorts propelled her into the shower, and one of them pulled the handle attached to the chain. The water that spurted gloriously over her was luke-warm, clear, clean. She wallowed in it, enjoying its cool touch, its massaging action on her sore shoulder muscles. The water ran for about three minutes, and then stopped.

'Damn,' she muttered under her breath. There was the melodius sound of laughter from the room behind her. She turned around. The little girl, Josie, had gone, and in her place were two more Polynesian beauties, younger than Miri, and equally under-dressed. They might have been twins—despite the fact that such a thing is considered terribly unlucky! The two newcomers chattered like a pair of magpies, and then stopped and giggled again. Miri gave some command. One of the smaller girls stepped out of her pareau and joined Rose in the shower. In a moment she was being soaped vigorously from head to foot.

'Moera and Leaha,' Miri called. 'They have no English. They are surprised that you are white all over, no? They never see such a thing before. They say you are plenty woman. The men will be mad for you, you understand!'

Not me, Rose thought grimly. I'm not joining the lust-parade on this damn island! All three of the Polynesians giggled again. Wondering, Rose looked down at herself. Her pale white skin was turning blush-red in some very embarrassing places. Damn! she muttered under her breath. The soaping was over. Miri pulled the handle of the chain again, and the water gushed as before, exactly three minutes, no more. She had always had a furtive hatred of her own slightly over-stated curves. Especially in the French society, where 'slender' and 'sleek' equated to beauty. Under the urging of Moera, she stepped out of the shower and into a huge warm towel. Both Miri and Leaha began a gentle massage, drying her off. They hissed in sympathy at the great black bruises on her shoulders, giggled as they dried her long blonde hair, holding its strands up beside their own raven-darkness for comparison.

When she was thoroughly dried they led her out back to the bedroom and gave her her first lesson in the use of the all-encompassing sheet of cloth that made a skirt, or, when folded differently, a sarong. One of the cloths they showed her was heavy, the other two very light. Colours splashed wildly in all of them. Miri had left them to go back to the kitchen. By dint of sign-language Rose asked the other two girls about the differences. Both giggled. 'This *tapa*,' Moera told her, pointing to the heavier material. 'Hard to make.' She made a movement indicating the pounding of fibres. 'This one,' she pointed to the lighter cloth, 'This Bir ming Ham.' And both of them seemed convulsed in giggles again. Rose shook her head, and no longer tried to repress her own smile.

The first *pareau* demonstration was a complete failure. They draped the cloth just above her hips, letting it fall gracefully to her ankles. It looked wonderfully sexy, but when she peered into the little wall-mirror, all she could see was her breasts, standing proudly unsupported. 'Too much,' she sighed, and tried her sign-language again.

The sarong was just a little better. Tied over her breasts, with both shoulders bare, it dropped to just below her knees. But the knot bothered her. She had often worn bath towels in this manner, and could not easily forget how little force it took to disengage them. Finally, against the objections of the pair, she devised a draping that went over her shoulder, much like a Roman toga, with the bottom falling half-way down her thighs. She smiled her thanks to the two girls. They left the room, looking too sombre to be true. She offered a grateful word in her Louisiana French. Moera looked back at her, shook her head, and said *'Aita e pe'ape'a.'* He came into the room as they went out.

She pirouetted to demonstrate her mastery of the fashion. 'Good,' he chuckled. 'But you won't get away with it. Everyone will laugh, you know.'

'No, I don't know,' she snapped. 'What did Moera say when she went out?'

'Aita e pe'ape'a?' he repeated. 'Loosely translated, it means "it ain't no big thing".'

'And why will everybody laugh?'

'Because you've got the customs backward,' he laughed. Tears actually formed in his eyes. 'You cover your breasts. In the outer islands the old customs still hold. If you've got 'em, show 'em!'

'Well—I don't intend to be a peepshow,' she snapped at him. Her legs were growing shaky. She felt behind her for a chair, and dropped into it. He could sense that she was disturbed, and grew solemn. 'But that's only half of it,' he sighed. 'In Tahiti you show the breasts, but never—never—never—do you show the inside of the thighs above the knee. To be frank, my dear, you are now indecently dressed!'

'Damn you all!' The tears came too readily. She struggled to pull down the hem of the *pareau*, with little success.

'Hey,' he offered soothingly. 'You've done well so far. Keep your chin up, my dear. We trying to get liquids into you, not out. Hungry?'

For some stupid reason he sounded so reasonable that the tears dried up. She dabbed at her eyes with her knuckles. He whipped a huge white handkerchief out of the pocket of his disreputable shorts. 'Always carry one for stray weeping women,' he intoned.

She snatched at it, more to hide her expression than to dry her eyes. Do you really, she thought. Altogether too well trained, aren't you. Where's your wife, I wonder? 'I guess I must be hungry,' she stammered. 'I guess I could eat a little bit.'

'That's the way,' he returned. 'A little now, a little later. In a couple of days you'll be completely well. How long were you in that raft?'

Her mind snapped to attention. Trick question number one gets simple answer number one! 'I don't remember any raft,' she said cautiously. 'Was I in a raft?'

'No, not to my knowledge.' He answered quickly, as if trying to cover up some *faux pas*. 'I was thinking of something else. You can't remember a thing?'

'Not a thing. Do you know who I am?'

'Yes.' Nothing more than that. No embellishments. It's like talking to a stone, she told herself fiercely. But before she could rephrase her question, Miri came in with a tray.

'Sit over here,' he directed, arranging a small stool adjacent to a rickety table. The native girl balanced the tray gracefully while he cleared the mess of papers and books, then set it down. 'Help yourself,' he commanded.

The food was set out on wooden platters. There were no utensils. Nothing seemed familiar, everything smelled good. He watched, smiling, and then began to identify things.

'Fish here,' he pointed to one corner of the platter, where little squares of white meat were piled up. 'And sauce over there. Dip the fish in the sauce and have at it.'

'What kind of fish?' She was busy at the work. The little cubes were hard to handle, but the sauce was spicy, tasty. She essayed five or six pieces, then stopped to lick her fingers.

'Bonito,' he told her. 'We live off the sea. The Bonito run in the channel between our island and Maupiti. Like it?'

'It's delicious,' she chuckled, digging in for another piece. 'How is it cooked?'

'Cooked? It's not,' he returned. Her hand stopped in mid-motion. His eyes lit up in glee.

'Some joke,' she snapped at him. 'Raw fish? What's this?'

This was a concoction that looked like fried potatoes. 'Breadfruit,' he told her. 'Fried in coconut oil. It has no real flavour of its own, but it's highly nutritional. Give it a try.'

She did. It had a bread-like taste, crunchy, with some pleasant flavouring which she could not identify. He filled her glass with a thin white liquid. 'And this?' she enquired.

'Coconut milk,' he said. 'We've run out of powdered milk, and there's no dairy business on the island. If you get thirsty for real milk, we'll fly over to Papeete one day.'

Like hell we will, she shouted to herself. Fly over to
Papeete? Back out of the frying pan and into the jail.
You don't catch me that quickly, Mister whoever you
are! And while I'm on that subject: 'You never did tell
me your name,' she pouted.

'Name? Oh, *my* name. It's Gendron. Giles Gendron.
Pretty soon you'll know it as well as your own.' He was
trying to make a joke out of it. And amnesiacs probably
never see the humour of things like that, she told
herself. It took but a second to concoct a dismal face.

'Or probably forget as quickly as I have my own,' she
returned. He had the grace to blush.

'I'm sorry,' he apologised. 'I keep forgetting. Have
you had enough for now?'

'I—I think I have,' she stuttered, 'but there's still this
—this grey paste on the plate. What's that?'

He bent over her shoulder to look. 'Well, I'll be
darned. The kitchen help is putting on the dog for you,
my dear. That's *poi*. It's a special paste made from taro
roots. Very popular. Hardly ever lasts past the kitchen
door, it's so good. Taste it with two fingers. Like this.'
He demonstrated, twirling two fingers together in the
mixture, pulling them out, and hastily shoving them
into his mouth.

'You have to move fast. Good *poi* is thick enough not
to drip away, but just barely.'

She gave it a successful try. 'And that's good *poi*?'

'It is if you like it. *Poi* is an acquired taste.'

'I like it.'

'Well, don't let it go to your head,' he laughed,
coming over to her stool to stand close behind her. 'It
might help if you stretch your legs a bit.' He offered an
arm. She struggled to her feet, but dizziness assailed
her, whirling her off balance, weak kneed. He snatched
her up before she fell, and slipped her back into her
bed. She managed a weak 'thank you' before her eyes
closed.

For two more days they plied her with food and drink, and then he was back again. 'Now we walk,' he commanded. Her legs moved stiffly, and her upper calves complained, but she moved—out of the bedroom, into the hall.

'Bedrooms to the right. Three of them.' He gestured. 'So they get the morning sun. On this side, the dining room, my workroom. That back alley leads to the kitchen. It's a separate building.'

He led her through a double set of screen doors, and out on to a broad veranda that completely surrounded the house. 'This is the place where we do most of our living,' he said.

She sank thankfully into a lounge chair which he pulled up for her, and looked around. 'It—it catches my breath,' she said happily, and gave him her best smile. She was looking east, into the morning sun. The house was situated on a rise of ground, about five hundred feet from the end of a narrow bay. A pair of mountains, twins they looked to be, guarded either side of the bay. A long gleaming white beach in the shape of a huge V spread beside the green water. The bay opened on to a reef-sheltered lagoon. A half-mile out a narrow channel cut through the reef, and into the deep blue of the pacific waves, smashing in white fury on the coral. At the near end of the bay a small stream poured down from the mountain behind them. To her right, two more mountains blocked the view to the west.

'*Pakuo*,' he pointed. 'That's the bay. The river is called *Papetahemaitai*—if you've breath enough to say it, that is. The mountains guarding the mouth of the bay are Mona Aui, and Mona Atau. The pair to your westward are what give the island its name. *Te Tuahine*. The Sisters.'

'And the one behind the house?' She had swung herself out over the rail of the veranda, looking up at the towering broken peak behind them.

'I can't tell you that,' he laughed. 'That's Pele's mountain. The Goddess of the Volcano, you know. There's a secret name that only the *tahu'a* knows. But everybody else, they just pretend there's no mountain there. We're all Christians here. Nobody believes in the old gods, that's for sure. Nevertheless, nobody goes up Pele's mountain except the old priest—the *tahu'a*. And all that on an island two miles across and eight deep.'

It was too much for her to absorb. She was still tired. Her bones racked and ached. A brace of coconut palms stood sentry in front of the house. Generals of the coconut army, she mused. Down behind the beach a whole army of them stood, while in the wetlands at the delta of the river, bamboo shoots swayed in the breeze. A tiny paradise, the mountains, the beaches, the wild growth of papaya, breadfruit, banana. And flowers beyond description, birds of brilliant colour. All marvellous.

'It seems like paradise,' she sighed.

She could hear the shouting of children at play from just around the curve of the bay. A cluster of thatched huts marked a village in the distance. The breeze was laden with gardenia, vanilla, lemon, oranges. 'All perfect,' she told him.

'And yet—not really,' he returned. 'Up until thirty-five years ago nobody lived here. There was no entrance into the lagoon. Te Tuahine has the one thing most pacific islands lack—water. But there was no way to get at it. And then the French government took over Murumura—at the other end of this island chain—as a test site for their nuclear weapons. The people here were re-settled from Murumura. It cost a fortune to blast a passage through the reef, and here you see the results.'

'And you? What brought you here?'

It was the wrong question. She could see the tiny muscles at the side of his mouth flicker, and a curtain came down over his face. She wished desperately that she might recall the question, but she wanted to know so badly. 'Should I not have asked that?' she pleaded. He seemed to be staring into the distance, watching the frigate birds making their way back from the deep ocean.

'Oh, it's a legitimate question,' he sighed.

'For which you don't have a legitimate answer?'

He smiled over at her. 'Dead hit,' he chuckled. She relaxed against the back of her chair, returning his smile. Things seemed to be so much—nicer—when he smiled. It was almost as if he had daemons to dispell, and was human after all.

He seemed to be ready to say something else, when a huge Polynesian man came up the side of the hill, evidently using a set of stairs she could not see. He was a big man by birth, she noticed. And he carried a few extra pounds around the stomach, which bulged out of his tattered tan shorts. His feet were bare, a big straw hat perched on top of his jet black hair, and all the rest of him was sun-bronzed. Gendron got up and went to the edge of the porch. '*Iorana oe*.' He offered. 'I hear you got the sickness, Sam. You came home to get better?'

Big white teeth flashed at them both. 'You know it,' Sam roared. 'Five years I work. Good pay. Carry the loads, drive the truck, keep the accounts. Hey, I do pretty good for a Kanaka boy, no?'

'Until you catch *fiu*, huh?'

'Just so. Until I catch *fiu*.' The Polynesian struggled up on to the porch and dropped uninvited into one of the bamboo chairs. It complained under his weight.

'You've been sick, Mr—Sam?' Rose felt the need to say something. He didn't *look* sick. Who could be sick in Paradise? 'Is it something infectious?' Both men roared in laughter. She could feel the blush spreading across her face.

'I didn't think it was all *that* funny,' she said coldly.

'Of course not,' Gendron comforted her. 'We beg your pardon. It's the disease that's funny, not anything you said. *Fiu* is the disease of boredom. When a Polynesian has had enough of doing some one thing, then he gets *fiu*—he walks off and leaves it all behind him. Mr Apuka has been working with the French nuclear organisation, the CEP. And now he's come home. That was some party the other night, Sam.'

'*Aue*,' the big man grinned at him. 'Too bad you don't come, Giles, we stay five, maybe six, hours on the beach. Plenty of roast pig, plenty of fish, plenty of beer. And then we dance—lord how we dance. I don't go home until all the beer is gone. And how you feel, little lady? You have a rough time.'

'I—I feel all right,' she stammered. 'Mr—Giles—has taken good care of me—and the girls too, of course. But I—I just don't remember anything!' There, she thought fiercely. Get your excuses in early and then let them chew on that! But Sam seemed not the least bit surprised. He nodded, flashed that broad smile, and turned to Giles.

'That liferaft,' he suggested. 'Young Fatara. He thinks to marry, you know. He comes to me today. He got his hut, but he lose his boat in the storm, no? So what you think we give him the raft, he can use it to fish in the lagoon, at least. Nice young man.'

'Good idea,' Giles returned. Rose was facing away from him as he spoke, but his tone drew her eyes back to his face. He was making some sort of signal to Apuka—some wiggling of the fingers, arching of the eyebrows. Now what, she asked herself? Does he feel some sort of guilt, giving away my raft like that. She was about to make a comment when a thought suddenly struck her. Amnesiacs certainly wouldn't recall the existence of a rubber raft! Even though they had ridden one of them for days on end! She ducked her head and looked back out to sea again.

'Mr Apuka,' she asked softly. 'Are you the chief in this area?'

'Me?' He laughed, every portion of his body shaking. 'No more chiefs,' he finally gasped. 'The *Ali'i* all gone, lady. No more *mana*, no more nobles—all gone. And pretty soon all the Polynesians go *pau*. Too many Chinese, too many Malay, too many French. And now, too many tourists. Pretty soon we are like Hawaii— everybody *tamarii afa*. Mixed breeds. Is not bad, you understand. The most beautiful vahines must have some *Tinito* blood. *Nehenehe*, them. All beautiful.'

'And you don't mind?'

'*Aue*, lady, everybody minds, but nobody does nothing. Only the *tahu'a*—the priest—only the *tahu'a* cries in the mountain.'

'The old religion still lives in places?'

Sam chuckled at her ignorance. 'The first white man comes to stay on the island is British missionary,' he said. 'Before the French. Long before. We all belong Church of England. You come to church sometime and you see. Hey, I gotta go. *Parahi*.'

She watched him go, feeling the strangeness of what she had seen and heard. It brought her back to her own problems. She needed to know much—so very much—before this Paradise could be a refuge. Sooner or later the police would come. Native police, of course. Tahiti was now self-governing, with its own elected officials, and France controlled only its external relations.

'I need to know,' she told him. 'I need to know who I am, where I am, and what's going on. I need to know. Desperately.' She sank back in her chair and gave thanks for her training in dramatics. 'And why all this looks familiar.'

'You don't remember a thing?'

'Nothing!' He seemed to be assessing her again. And then he took his decision.

'We came here three years ago,' he said. 'I'm a writer. This is a good place for writing. Josie takes school lessons by correspondence. There's a place in Maryland that specializes in educating overseas Americans. I don't want to tell you much more. I talked by radio to a doctor in Tahiti yesterday. He tells me that your memory will come back on its own, and that prodding you will cause harm.'

'But I *have* to know at least who I am. You *do* know, don't you?'

'Oh yes, I know all about you,' he laughed. He leaned across the wicker table that separated them and tilted her head up. She was compelled to look into those dark brown eyes. It was like seeing a new world through a keyhole. There were flecks of gold in those depths, and a gleam—almost of desperation. Oh no, she screamed at herself. He can't really know—can he? Was he calling the police on that radio? Telling them that he knew where Rose Lambert was hiding? No! She almost screamed the denial aloud, but barely managed to restrain it.

He was fumbling with her right hand. She looked down, terror-stricken, to watch. He was slipping a wide gold ring on to the third finger of her left hand.

'You left it in the bathroom,' he said softly. His eyes were glued to hers. 'You're my wife—Josie's mother.'

CHAPTER TWO

SHE managed to get back to her room just after sundown. The long afternoon had worn down her feeble reserves. It had been a light dinner. Smoked fish, *mahimahi*, Miri insisted, although it looked a lot like tuna. A salad of sweet mango accompanied it, garnished with nuts, and a sprinkling of grated coconut. Tea was served.

'It's one of our major difficulties,' Giles told her as she cradled the warm cup in her hand. 'Coffee is too expensive. We have it for a week or two after the supply boat comes in, and then it's back to tea. Tea is not only cheaper, but easier to come by. Wine is almost impossible. Beer somewhat less so. But we do have plenty of water, and that's something you can't say about most Pacific islands. None of the atolls in our chain have underground water. And even Maupiti, our neighbouring island, lives entirely from rain-water. Nice in the wet season; not so nice in the dry.'

And then he had taken her arm and gently escorted her to her room. There was a sort of caress in his voice as he turned her around at the door, kissed her gently, and walked away down the hall. She was alone for the first time that day.

What in the world is he up to? She threw herself down on the bed wearily, determined to reason it all out. I'm a faker. He thinks I have amnesia—I hope. That's *my* game. But what the devil is *his* game? He must surely believe the story I gave him, otherwise he would hardly dare to try that one on. 'You're my wife!' Indeed! Have I come across some sex-starved Crusoe? It hardly seems possible.

The place swarms with good-looking native girls—

and I'll bet a dime to a doughnut that he wouldn't have to whistle up a storm to get one of them into his bed!

And then the little girl. Josie Gendron, no less. Why, the child looks more like me than she does like him! But he *says* he's her father, and she seems to agree. Or is he the con man *par excellence*, who not only has the child believing that she's his, but now wants to convince me that I'm his wife? Walk softly, Rosie, she sighed to herself. If only Papa were here—just to listen to me tell it. Would he ever get a laugh!

Poor Papa. I *have* to believe that he escaped the wreck. We've always been so close. There's always been a bond between us, no matter what the distance—and I *know* it's not broken. I can feel it still! Lord, keep Papa safe. And with that thought she fell into a deep and troubled sleep. Which was just as well for her state of mind, for she missed the entire conference in the kitchen.

'Look, it's the only way,' Giles said to the group. He was still in his tattered shorts, but had thrown on a light cotton T-shirt against the cool of the night. He ran a worried hand through his thatch of hair. Sam Apuka was there, along with Miri, the other two Polynesian girls, and little Josie. 'She doesn't remember a thing. It's not an uncommon happening. There's no identification on her or on the raft. All we have to do is keep her confused for a few days—a week at most. Somebody is pressuring the Tahiti government to take action. And the police judiciary mean to send an inspector to see for himself.'

'You think they would have forgotten, no?' Sam stretched himself and yawned. 'Me, I need a good night of sleep. How come they don't forget? It all happen three—four years ago.'

'Because my former wife has sworn to a charge of kidnapping,' Giles said disgustedly. 'My own child, and they charged me with kidnapping.'

'But you didn't kidnap me,' Josie pleaded. 'I asked you to come and get me. Don't that count?'

'No,' her father sighed. 'You're a minor. The court gave you into your mother's custody after the divorce.'

'Crazy, these Americans,' Sam said. 'She don't want the kid, no? How come she keeps trying to track you down?'

'So I couldn't have her,' Gendron replied bitterly. 'Just so I couldn't have her.' His fingers clutched into fists as he pounded on the table-top. Hold your temper down, he ordered himself. Blowing your top, that's what got you into this damn mess. Be diplomatic! But his heart and mind could not agree.

'So you kidnap your own kid, and you run to Samoa, but that's too close to American law, and you come to Te Tuahine? How come.'

'Because the French-Tahitian law isn't all that easy on extradition, damn it. There's a lot more respect for the child's rights in these islands!'

'Ah, but now she knows you are somewhere in French Polynesia? How come she know that?'

'Private detectives,' Gendron snorted. 'I pay her plenty of alimony. She uses it to hire detectives. And to support that no-goodnik she's living with.' The bile rose in his throat at the thought. I should have killed the bastard, he told himself.

'Aha. She lives with another man? How come they don't get married? Then the kid have a mother and father. That's the best.'

'How come they don't get married?' There was a sharp cynical snap to his voice. 'Because if she marries again she loses all the alimony. What else? She likes the sound of money. And a bird in the hand is worth two in the bush?'

'Huh?' Sam chuckled. 'What bird we talkin' about?'

'The money bird,' Miri interrupted. 'What is past makes no difference. Giles is here. Josie is here. Now we need to keep them here.'

'Okay, okay. I just try to understand.' Sam shifted his not inconsiderable weight in his chair. 'Just tryin' to understand. And I don't need no *vahine* to explain. Was a time when everybody knows his place. Those were the good times!'

'Are you that old?' Miri was laughing at him with her eyes, but trying her best to look respectful. And not succeeding.

'Someday,' Sam threatened, 'you gonna meet a real *tane*—a real man—who set you straight. You see!'

'Not you, old man. Not you!' Miri was laughing, and Moera quickly joined her. Apuka glared at them both, and then joined in. Polynesians love to laugh, even at themselves.

'So why not give the child back to her mother,' Sam asked, when the gale had passed. 'Any girl better off with her mother. Always.'

'Not always,' Giles interrupted grimly. 'Not always.'

'I don't wanna go back,' Josie said. 'I *won't* go back! That man—he kept touching me. I told my mother, but she just laughed. Said it was just in fun. I didn't think so. He likes to hurt people. So I called my Dad. And he came and got me, and they had a terrible fight. I'm not gonna go back. No way!'

'Well,' Sam said reflectively, '*popa'a* ways very funny. I never understand at all. Better here on the island. All the children belong to all the people, always. Nobody hurts children. Never! So what we do now?'

'The way I figure it,' Giles said softly, so softly that they all seemed to cling together conspiratorially, 'We convince this little lady that she's Josie's mother. We really get her to believe it. So when the inspector arrives, he finds me and my child—and my wife—all perfectly happy together. We'll have to shuffle a few truths, of course. Josie—you're only six years old, remember.'

'But I'm nine—almost ten, Daddy.'

'We're playing a game, Josie. An important game. You are six years old. This little lady is your mother. You were born here on the island. Can you fix the church records, Sam?'

'Sure. Easy. Nobody keeps record all the time. Just once in a while, when somebody feel like it, then we enter everything we can remember. Births, deaths, weddings, typhoons, like that.'

'Fine. And you, Miri, you tell the rest of the women. Everybody must be told. Don't miss a soul.'

'Ah—Giles.' Sam had a sudden afterthought. 'It ain't gonna work if we don't tell the *tahu'a*. And for sure he have to go up the mountain, to tell Pele. No doubt about that.'

'Oh God! I'd forgotten him!' Giles threw back his head in disgust, ran his fingers through his hair in a nervous reaction, and returned to the debate. 'We *have* to tell him. That crazy old priest and his volcano goddess? Surely you can control him?'

'Hey,' Sam rumbled. 'The old religion is gone, no? But the old habits, they ain't gone. We tell the *tahu'a*. He goes up the mountain and tells Pele—and then everything goes okay!'

'I don't know about that, Sam. He and I have had some pretty tough arguments.' For just an instant Giles felt the cold hand of defeat resting on his shoulders. But whatever was to be done, had to be done here. They had run too fast, Josie and he. There was just no place else to run. It *had* to work. This little woman was the key to success— a gift from God, so to speak. It *had* to work. 'Okay,' he sighed. 'I'll tell the *tahu'a*. Now, how about everybody to bed and get some *tooto*. We all have a lot to do tomorrow.'

He watched them all go. He was tired, mentally tired. His daughter slipped a hand in his, and they laughed as they watched Miri and Sam leave together. Despite their arguments, and a fifteen year difference in age, the two were attracted to each other.

His daughter tugged him out on to the veranda. There was a half-moon, low and silvery in the sky, lighting a path across the calm Pacific. The stars seemed close enough to touch. Sirius, Tahiti's own navigational star, stood quietly overhead. The only sound was the lulling sigh of the waves touching gently on the beach. A heavy musk of vanilla, hibiscus, orange, and ocean salt came down the wind. It rattled the paper-thin leaves of the bougainvillaea. The faint sound of voices drifted up to them from the village. Happy voices.

'You think we can fool them all?' Josie asked. 'All of them?'

'We can if we try, love.' He ruffled her skein of soft golden hair. 'You don't want to go back to New York, and I don't want to lose you. All we have to do is convince this woman. And both of us have to work hard at it. Can we?'

'I—I don't know, Daddy. I'll try. What's her name?'

'Lord, I'd forgotten that,' he sighed. 'I'll think of something.'

'And she can't tell us, can she?'

'It is a mess, isn't it,' he chuckled, picking the little girl up and cuddling her close to him. 'Why do we two always seem to get into these stupid messes? Come on now—you're up late for a six-year-old.'

'Daddy! I'm—oh, it's the game, isn't it. I hafta remember. Yes, I'm up late for a six-year-old. Are you gonna tuck me in and tell me a story?'

'I surely am, baby. All about the little girl who was eaten by the *tiaporo* because she forgot her lines.'

'You're just making that up,' the little girl laughed. 'Devils don't eat little girls. Only boys!'

'Okay, okay smarty. Off to bed with you.'

He followed her down the corridor to the bathroom in the far back of the house, and then to her bedroom, squeezed in between his own and that of their guest. What the devil is the woman's name? We have to call her something—something that won't upset her.

'When do we start the play?' Josie whispered to him after he had shushed her, pointing a finger next door. 'Tomorrow?'

'I suppose so, sweetheart,' he murmured, tucking the single sheet over her slight form. Her night gown is too small for her, he mused. Everything is too small for her. I just can't seem to find the time to see to everything. And I just can't see her running around like the native kids. What am I, some kind of inverted snob? He sat beside the girl's bed, holding her hand, until her steady breathing demonstrated that she had dropped off to sleep. He disentangled her fingers from his own, lay the tiny arm down on top of the sheet, and tiptoed out.

Start the play tomorrow? He paused by the doorway where the castaway girl lay. The almost-transparent curtain blew in the wind. She was muttering something in her sleep. He brushed the curtain aside, and went in. The moon, shining brilliantly through the two windows, provided plenty of light. She was tossing and turning on the bed, the words she muttered too indistinct to make sense. He moved closer to the bed and bent over the tossing form. The sheet had slipped completely off her shoulders, and she was sleeping nude. He gasped as the silver moon painted the fullness of her breasts, the tiny waist, the burgeoning hips. He leaned closer. 'Papa! Papa! It's me, Rose!' There were tears streaking her cheek.

Oh Lord, he thought, what now? She was shaking, quivering, and instead of inspiring pity she stirred him erotically. 'Damn,' he whispered under his breath. 'Another minute and she'll wake up the house!' It was only an excuse, but he seized on it avidly, discarding his shorts and climbing into the wide bed with her. As his arms came around her she seemed to welcome them, moving close to him, cuddling her forehead on his neck, so that the fragrance of her hair filled his nostrils.

The weight of her breast fell on his chest. He sucked in a startled breath, and then, unable to control himself, let his hand drift down until it cupped the soft fullness of her. A rush of feelings swept over him, feelings he had not experienced in years. Lust and nostalgia, he told himself grimly, but his fingers climbed the mountain of desire, and her bronze tip stiffened under his questing touch.

She had fallen into a turbulent dream. The tiny yacht was almost standing on beams end as the force of the typhoon toyed with it, forced it closer in on the rocky shore of Moorea, where the great stone fangs reached out to them. She had been sleeping nude. She snatched at her life jacket and ran. A thunderous crash upended her world and sent her sliding the length of the small cabin and out into the open cockpit. 'Papa! Papa!' she yelled into the wind. 'It's me, Rose!'

The strong warm arms came around her, cradling her safe from the ravening ocean. She snuggled in closer. There had been many a close scrape for them, she and her father, and in every case his fertile mind had brought them through safely. There was no need to fear. Until suddenly a huge hand trailed fingers down her shoulder and took up the weight of her heavy breast!

Her eyes snapped open. The wild night at sea disappeared. Silver moonlight painted a bamboo room in a bamboo house, and the warmth of a very male body squeezed close up against her. Her mind fumbled, having trouble sorting reality from dream. And the hand that held her breast in thrall squeezed gently.

She had only one hand free. The other was trapped between their two bodies. That free hand came around, fist clenched, and smashed into the shadowed face. 'What the hell,' he muttered, startled. But his grip relaxed. She rolled away from him like an enraged cat, spitting her anger as she landed on the floor on hands and knees, and then scrambled up to wedge herself protectively into a corner of the room.

'What the devil do you think you're doing,' she hissed at him. 'Get out of here you—you——'

'Husband,' he supplied affably. 'I'm your husband, Rose. What else?' He sat up in the bed, his back against the headboard, the sheet crumpled down to his waist. 'Surely you don't think that we found Josie in a bush?'

She was startled into frozen silence. Oh my God. The 'husband' routine! He thinks that I believe that? But if I tell him the honest truth I'll be blowing my own cover. Selective amnesia is too much for me to struggle with. It was all or nothing. Damn the man! Taking full advantage of me, isn't he. What a rotten arrogant—

'Rose?' And he knows my name? Another part of the crazy game that he's trying to play? Well, I really have no choice, do I! That jail in Papeete is the worst I've ever seen. I couldn't possibly survive for a day locked up in that place!

'I—maybe,' she sighed. 'You say so. I—I don't remember. I just don't remember—Giles. You can't—you just can't jump into my bed and think that I'll welcome—you just can't do that! How can I know for sure that you're my husband, when I don't even remember you?'

He stirred against the headboard, putting his face into shadows. 'Believe me, Rose,' he said softly. 'How would I know your name otherwise? Or that you have a mole on your right buttock. How?'

'I don't know,' she answered despondently. Her mind ran at full speed. How does he know? The mole, of course, because he had his hand—oh, Lord, this is too impossible to be happening! Why don't I just give up and tell him the truth? Or why don't I fight back? Why should he have it the easy way? I just can't give up to *him*. It would only take him ten minutes to discover that I'm just another stupid virgin. Damn the man!

Why don't I remember him? What would a real
amnesiac feel about—and the idea struck her full in the
face.

She grappled behind her on the chair for her *pareau*,
winding it around her in sarong fashion, and then
returned to the attack. 'Why don't I remember you,
Giles,' she asked softly, almost whispering. 'Is it
because I don't want to remember you? Why do I have
all these bruises, all these cuts? Is that why I don't want
to remember you? Because you did all this to me? Beat
me up, did you? Is that how you get your kicks? Why
else would your wife not want to remember you? Giles?'

He swung himself up off the bed in one swift motion,
a dark shadow now, with the moon over-swept by high
clouds. She tried to back away from him, but his hands
trapped her shoulders. She winced as they closed on her
bruises, but it was too dark for him to see her face. His
hands shook her gently.

'No, damn it, I didn't lay a finger on you,' he
snapped. 'It was—well, I can't tell you what happened.
And you *are* my wife!' The bitterness, the dark threat
behind the words, sent a shiver down her spine.

'Daddy?' The little voice from next door broke in on
them. 'Daddy? Is something wrong?'

'No, baby,' he reassured. 'I was just talking with your
mother.'

'Oh? Mommy? You didn't come to say good night to
me, Mommy!'

'Well?' he hissed at her. 'Doubt me all you want, but
the little girl believes—and she needs you! So you don't
remember me—or anything else, for that matter. But
Josie loves you, and I won't have anything done to
upset her—not anything, do you hear?'

'I—I——" She was at a loss for words. She who had
the gift of gab from the Irish half of her family. Not a
word could she get out. It wasn't just the man. A
consummate con man he was, but the little girl was in

as deeply as he! How in the world can a girl that age play me up like this?

'Well?' His lips were inches from her ear. The sibilant sound rattled around inside her head, adding to her confusion.

'All right,' she whispered. 'I'll try to do what I can— with the girl, mind you. Not with you! I don't want you near me, you understand? Not until I remember!' And that will be a cold day in Hell, she assured herself.

'Just don't forget,' he returned. 'Play it up.'

'I'll do my best,' she whispered. And then, a little more loudly, 'I'll come now, Josie. I must have fallen asleep too early.' Then, back to the whisper, 'Turn me loose, you——'

'Loving husband,' he interjected. 'Come on, we'll both go and say good night to the child.' One of his hands came around and patted her in a proprietary manner on her bottom. She flinched away from him, and started towards the door, outraged.

'You never used to be so hard to hold,' he chuckled, as he followed her into the corridor and down to the next room. Like hell I wasn't, she swore at him under her breath. Like hell I wasn't! But the cold image of the jail in Papeete flashed into her mind. She forced the rest of her feelings into a dark corner of her mind, fixed a smile on her face, and went in to say good night to her *daughter*.

He stood back from the bed while the two of them exchanged a hug and a kiss, and only came up to the bed after Rose had carefully rearranged the pillows, straightened out the sheets, and planted another kiss on the little girl's forehead.

'Don't forget to kiss Daddy!' Heaven protect us, he thought, she's padding her part. If she over-does the whole affair—oh Lord. Although it looks as if we have Miss Rose—Mrs Rose—in a spot she can't wiggle out of! Now, give us a couple of days to spread the word around the island, and let the inspector come and do his worst!

'Daddy?'

'What, baby?'

'You didn't kiss Mommy.'

'Oh. You mean now?'

'Of course now. I can't sleep if you don't.'

The child had the bit in her teeth, he thought. Shakespeare could have used a kid like this! And she wasn't going to give up until it was done her way.

Warily his hands spanned Rose's waist and turned her to face him. She had her head bowed. The long silky hair hid her expression as she stood passively under his hands. Come on, co-operate, he wished at her. She might have sensed the message. Her face turned up towards his, just as the moon escaped the clutches of the clouds and sprayed the room with silver again. A quiet oval face, a beautiful complexion. A Mona Lisa smile on those full lips. Oh well, in for a dollar, he told himself. Make it look good!

He stooped to her, lightly touching his lips to hers. Warm, moist lips, slightly parted. Make it long enough to be effective, he warned himself. And then suddenly the tip of her tongue touched his, the warmth evaporated into boiling cauldrons of wild feeling that sent streaks of flame up and down his spine. His arms tightened around her involuntarily, as he pressed closer to taste the sweet fire of her. Her breasts, hardly hidden under the thin cotton of the *pareau*, flattened against the muscles of his chest. He pulled her even closer. Her arms arched up around his neck. The room disappeared, faded into the background as he gasped for breath, then plunged into the maelstrom again. He shifted his target, nibbling on the tip of her ear. She moaned, scraped sharp nails down his shoulder blade and then suddenly seemed to recover, struggling to push him away.

He released her reluctantly. Her hands flashed immediately to the slipping knot of her pareau. And then, as if she were completely exhausted, she leaned forward against him, and almost slipped to the floor. He swept her up in his arms.

'Wow!' the little girl said.

'Wow is right,' he gasped, still short of breath. 'Go to sleep you little monster. *Tooto maitai.* Sleep well.'

'Is Mommy asleep?'

'I don't think so, love, but almost.'

'Did I do well, Daddy?'

'You did fine, baby. Go to sleep now. I have to carry Mommy back to her own bed. And you be sure to be quiet. She needs her rest.'

Yes, I surely do, Rose warned herself. Keep the eyes closed. Get your pulse-rate back to normal. You're an amnesiac. You don't remember anything. Especially you don't ever remember being kissed like *that* before! Feel the strength of those arms! You'd think I weighed only as much as his daughter. Keep those eyes closed! You're asleep, remember? If he kisses you like that again you're a lost soul, Rose Lambert!

'Rose?' He cuddled her closer, urging a response. She fought with all her willpower to deny it. Carefully, gently, he stretched her out on her bed, pulled the sheet over her, and dropped a feather of a kiss on her forehead.

'*Iorana,*' he whispered in her ear.

I wonder what that means, she asked herself as she heard his footsteps fading into the distance. He told me once, and I've really forgotten. I wonder what that means?

CHAPTER THREE

THE sun came up in a violent mood, sparking reds and blues and yellows off the clouds to the east of the island. One moment it was pitch dark. In another there was a line of green light along the horizon. Then for about fifteen minutes the skies were rampant with colour. And then the sun vaulted up, and the tropical day had begun. She leaned carefully against one of the bamboo posts that held up the roof of the veranda. For the first time since coming ashore on the island she felt—not entirely well, perhaps—but comfortable enough to make do for herself.

She had been wakened by the raucous clamour of the frigate birds as they headed seaward for their first meal of the day. Behind them the herring gulls were lined up to dive-bomb the lagoon. In the palm grove just in front of the house a pair of Golden Plover were disputing housing rights with a pure-white tern. The scene from her window had drawn her irresistibly. She swept up her *pareau*, knotted it carefully over her breasts, made sure that it fell decorously to her knees, and padded barefoot out of the house. She stood there at the steps and breathed deeply, loving the clean wet smell of the ocean, clear and unpolluted, as it no longer was on Tahiti, the Big Island.

The early-morning sounds of nature filled her ears, and so she was startled when a small hand slipped into hers. 'Mamma?' She looked down at the tousled blonde head, the too-short night gown, the big smile.

'Good morning Josie. Did you sleep well?'

The child was having difficulty, thinking in English, trying to express herself in French, with an occasional

Polynesian word thrown in. 'I slept well, Mamma. Did you have breakfast?'

'Not yet, love. I didn't want to wake anybody up.'

'You wouldn't of,' the little girl teased. 'Except for Daddy, that is. He likes to work in the nighttime, and he doesn't ever get up early in the morning. Moera is already in the kitchen, getting the breakfast ready. But now it's *vahines*' time at the beach. Come and swim?'

'I—I can't, Josie. I don't have a bathing suit.'

'But nobody wears a bathing suit, Mommy. Only girls can come to the beach until an hour after sunrise. It's the custom. And you always used to come swimming with me!'

There it goes again, Rose chided herself. Always. As if she and I had known each other all our lives. 'Always?' she teased.

'Well, always before you got sick. Please?'

'I——' but the look in those eyes, so much like her father's, could not be denied. Come on, Rose, she told herself. You heard the child. You and all the rest of the women on this crazy island go skinny-dipping every morning, right? You remember, Rose, don't you? And just for a moment it seemed all so real that she laughed.

Holding hands, they scrambled down the steps carved in the hill below the house. Simple steps, dug in shallow succession, walled with logs, that allowed them to set foot directly on the sparkling white sand of the beach. As Josie had said, across the river on the other side of the bay, several *pareau*-clad figures were running to the water. Watch, she commanded herself. Get it right the first time.

Across the bay the women barely hesitated, dropping their gaily-printed *pareaux* on the sand, and plunging into the quiet waters of the bay. And when in Rome, she asked herself? Josie had already slipped out of her tiny gown and was knee deep in the inviting water. Rose stood in the sand for an indecisive moment, shifting her weight from one foot to the other against the rising heat of the beach. And why do I have to be born the only prude in the family, she sighed. Her fingers climbed to the knot at her breast, paused there as she looked anxiously around, and the cloth fell to her feet.

She was off like a startled fawn, splashing out to thigh depth, then diving forward in a shallow racing dive, eager to get under the water. And not because it's cool and clean and inviting, she snapped to herself. Her head broke the surface almost half-way across this narrowest portion of the bay. Two sleek bronze forms ghosted by her in the other direction. One of the women raised her head just long enough for the traditional *'Iorana oe,'* before the dark head disappeared again. Rose floated lazily in place. 'Crazy language,' she muttered to herself. 'One phrase seems to mean everything. But I like what *he* said better. Live happily ever after!' She rolled over on her stomach, circling until she spotted Josie's little head plugging doggedly after her. Rose shook the water out of her eyes, porpoise-dived again, and glided back to enjoy the girl's company.

They raced and played and floated for another twenty minutes before the sound of a conch-shell trumpet disturbed the air. Almost immediately the *vahines* in the water streaked for shore, and were gone.

'We hafta go,' Josie shrieked at her, giggling. 'Now it's the men's turn. Hurry up, Mommy. It's *tapuu* to watch the men!'

'I'll bet it is,' Rose returned sarcastically. And I certainly won't, she told herself. But her head turned almost against her will, to snatch another look across the bay. And she was giggling as much as the little girl as she followed her around the head of the bay, struggling into her wet *pareau* as they went. Their new path skirted the marshes at the mouth of the little river, and then turned uphill.

'And where in the devil are we going now,' she finally gasped, as their way took them into the bamboo groves, and out of sight both of the house on the hill and the village by the sea.

'You'll see,' Josie teased. As indeed she did. Their final turn took them through heavy growth and out on to an earthen dam that created a pool of fresh water behind it.

The little girl, who was carrying her only garment in her hand, dropped it on the dam and jumped into the pool. 'I can't go all day with that salt on me,' she called back. 'Come on in. You'll be surprised.'

So I'll be surprised, Rose told herself almost hysterically. That's all I've been since the moment I landed on this island. Surprised, that is. Nobody wears any shirts, but everyone has something up their sleeves! Oh well. Once again her fingers struggled with the knot in her *pareau*, and the flimsy garment fell to the ground. The water looked deep enough, up to the level of Josie's neck, but it was too risky, this diving into unknown waters. So instead of diving she stepped off the edge of the dam, and promptly received her surprise. In the middle of the tropics, where the sun averaged ninety degrees or more on a normal day, the water bubbling merrily through the little pool was as cold as ice!

'Why you little monster!' she yelled as soon as she regained her breath. 'You're my daughter? What kind of a way is that to treat your mother? I'll get you for this, you little ——' And the ensuing chase, punctuated by laughter, was more than enough to give them both a thorough fresh-water rinse. They both stumbled out of the pool a few minutes later, and stretched themselves out on the top of the dam, panting.

And now's the time, Rose thought. The child is diverted. She won't be thinking carefully. I've got her in the right situation. She leaned closer to the shivering form. 'My, what big teeth you have,' she said. 'Are you really my daughter, Josie?'

But the girl was as elusive as quicksilver. 'Yes, of course I am,' she laughed. Both hands were behind her back, and there were crossed fingers on both.

They wasted minutes letting the sun dry them off. It didn't require a great deal of time. And it's not really wasted, Rose assured herself. Time is different here in the islands. There are long hours, and short hours. Only the stupid clock requires discipline and order. So finally they dressed, and wandered back hand-in-hand to the stairs that led up to the house. They stopped a quarter of the way up. An old man was coming down. As soon as she saw who it was Josie ducked behind the older woman and clutched at her for support.

'It's him,' the girl whispered. 'It's the *tahu'a!*' She didn't sound afraid of the old man—just cautious.

And he was an *old* man. Older than any Polynesian Rose had seen in her short three weeks in the islands. His face was over-run with wrinkles, his short hair was white, and tattoos covered both shoulders. He walked with the aid of a bamboo stick, but his proud body bent not an inch. A loin cloth and a little leather pouch strung around his neck on a leather thong was his complete attire. In his eighties, Rose thought, but look at the posture, the dignity of him! She stepped aside to give him room, feeling the absurd need to curtsey as he went by.

The old man noticed her instinctive gesture, smiled, and stopped. His cold steel eyes ran up and down her. There was a start—almost a look of surprise, as he examined her long blonde hair. His eyes shifted to the child's. When he spoke, his French was clumsy, as if it were something he had learned long ago, and never put to use.

'*Aue,*' he exclaimed softly. 'Apuka was right. *Te Tamahine a Tangora!*' He drew in his breath sibilantly through his teeth, and then, to Rose's amazement, switched to a very pedantic English. 'The Daughter of Tangora! Apuka was right!' Rose struggled with her breathing. Something about the old man left her unable to breathe regularly. And then he was gone, ambling down the stairs, leaning on his bamboo staff, muttering something under his breath.

'And what in the world was that all about,' Rose inquired as they resumed their climb.

'Don't ask me,' the suddenly subdued Josie returned. 'You can't expect a six year old kid to know everything!'

'Six years old? Come on, kid. Stop pulling my leg. You've got all your adult teeth.'

'So—so Papa says I'm—pre-something.'

'Precocious. I'll just bet you are, little miss. But I love you just the same.' And strangely enough, she told herself as they climbed on to the veranda, I think I mean it!

When they wandered into the dining room the breakfast table was set, and he was there. Somewhere behind them, in the cookhouse, a constant giggle accompanied the preparation of the meal.

'Ah, there you are,' he said as he got up. The little girl ran to him and hugged him. Then he stretched both hands out to Rose, pulled her to him, and kissed her forehead gently. 'Good morning love,' he offered softly.

'Good morning to you.'

She backed off warily, bumped into a chair, and slumped into it. Somehow or another this man was just too much. Someone to be feared. She could feel a little quiver of—fear—course down her spine. She folded her hands on the edge of the table and tried to look the prim prude that she knew she was.

Josie broke the ice. She scrambled up into her own chair, her tongue going a mile a minute, recounting everything. And I do mean everything, Rose reminded herself. Is there no way to turn her off?

'And your mother actually went swimming without her clothes?' The phrase penetrated her daze, and turned her blush-red.

'Of course,' his daughter returned as she dug into the tea and *firifiri*, the Tahitian equivalent of doughnuts. 'Everybody does. There's a lot of her, Daddy—ah, you know that anyway, don't you? She swims like a fish, and jiggles when she runs! I'm gonna be like her when I grow up!'

'Josie,' Rose snapped at her. 'That's not the kind of thing to talk about at the breakfast table!'

'Well, I'd really love to see her swim,' he laughed, heightening her confusion.

'You know you can't,' his daughter stated firmly. 'It's *tapuu*. You know that!'

'Yes, I guess I'll have to take your word for it then,' he laughed.

She tried desperately to find something to change the subject. *Firifiri*, of course. 'I'm surprised that we don't have croissants for breakfast,' she offered. 'In——' And you're about to give the whole game away, she shrieked at herself. She fumbled for an innocuous ending. 'I just thought that croissants were the French breakfast,' she stammered.

They both stared at her. 'You remember something?' he prodded.

'No,' she sighed. 'Just croissants, that's all.'

'Ah.' He seemed vastly relieved as he leaned back in his chair. It creaked as his weight changed. 'Yes. Of course. Croissants are the usual breakfast of the French. And you can get them in Tahiti, but not out here. Flour doesn't keep very well in the tropics. We *have* croissants, you know. For a couple of weeks after the quarterly supply boat comes in, we have a great many nice things.'

'The supply boat?' Again that quiver of alarm ran up her spine. A regular supply boat! Then there *was* communication between this speck in the Pacific and its neighbours. And sooner or later news would flow down that communications link!

'Yes,' he repeated. 'Four times a year, from Tahiti. We buy staples, and they take away our copra. Whenever anyone around here is willing to work at it, of course.'

'Oh!' They could both hear the tension in her voice. He decided to probe.

'In fact, it's due next week some time.' He offered the news casually, off-hand, but his eyes were glued to her face. She did her best to school her features. Her hair helped. As she ducked her head it swung around her face and hid her—for the moment—from his searching gaze. 'It will bring a surprise,' he continued. She ducked her head again. Oh God, not another surprise, she begged to herself.

'A police inspector is going to fly out to Maupiti, and the boat will bring him over,' he continued.

He didn't have to be a close observer to catch her reaction. Her head snapped up, the long strands of silky hair swirling around her throat. She was suddenly pale—completely white. Her eyeballs rolled up under their lids. She pushed her chair back from the table, upsetting the bowl in front of her, and staggered backwards.

He sat immobilised for just a moment, and then as she tottered, he was up beside her, just in time to catch her as she collapsed into his arms.

'I think your mother has fainted, baby,' he said quietly. 'Too much excitement, too soon.' He stood there with Rose in his arms, her fair hair tumbling over his shoulder, the sweet clean smell of her clogging his nostrils, sending those same quivering sensations up his arm, down his spine, that he had experienced the previous night. Dear God, he thought, can it really be just abstention? Look at her—almost an angel, with all her muscles relaxed, and that permanent look of fear hidden behind closed eyelids. I wonder who she really is. I wonder what the devil she's so afraid of? If I didn't need her so badly, I'd try to find ...

'You just gonna stand there, Daddy?' The little girl came over to his side and took one of Rose's drooping hands in her own. 'She's nice,' Josie whispered. 'I—I wish we could keep her for always. Daddy?'

'I'm going to take her into her room,' he snapped, using anger to suppress this other haunting feeling which he could not identify. 'See if Miri is in. We need some—oh, I don't know. There's a little vial of smelling salts in the first-aid kit. Ask Miri to bring it in, please.'

'You're not mad at me, are you?' Josie was trembling. 'I know I didn't do so good this morning. She doesn't believe I'm six years old. I told her you said I was a *precious* child——'

'Precocious,' he interrupted. 'No, I'm not mad at you, baby. At myself, yes but not you. Hurry up!'

He hurried down the hall with his burden, but at her bedside, was reluctant to put her down. The feeling of warmth as he held her close was the most pleasure he had experienced in many a day. Josie's right, he told himself. She's a whole lot of woman. Firm, yet soft. Curved the way Botticelli liked to paint them, warm and round. As I like them. Let's face it—as all red-blooded American men like them. Why did she faint? She looked well enough beforehand. Tired, perhaps, from the swimming? One minute lively and lovely, and then—bingo—she's out like a light.

Something to do with what I said? What the devil did I say? The supply boat is coming. How would that bother her. Unless? Unless there were others with her out there in the ocean. Somebody she loves—somebody dear to her, lost in that same storm. And she's afraid to find out whether it's true or not? And that's what is causing the amnesia? She's afraid to find out! She thinks the supply boat will bring in news of the wreck. I guess it must have been a wreck. And she doesn't want to know, so she's got amnesia! It all fits, just the way the doctor described it on the radio! Poor kid. Poor lovely beautiful kid!

He could hear the noise as multiple feet hurried down the hall. Carefully he stretched her out on top of the sheet, re-arranging the fall of her *pareau* at her knees to cover those beautiful thighs.

It took another fifteen minutes to coax her back out of the darkness. She came gently back, keeping her eyes closed until the last moment, and then gently feathering her lashes. He was her first sighting. She flinched away from him in the bed, and a cold hardness flashed across his face. Josie crowded in front of him, to be rewarded by a weak smile, all she could muster at the moment.

'Mommy? Are you all right?' The little girl threw both arms around Rose's neck and hugged her close.

'I'm all right,' she managed to get out. 'I'm all right. I think—maybe I just need something to eat, or something.'

'I'll get it right away,' Josie said. 'I'll make some fresh tea, and——'

'I'll make the tea,' Miri interrupted. Both of them hurried off on the same errand, leaving her alone in the room with him. He could hardly fail to notice that she edged over to the other side of the bed and struggled to get up.

'No,' he commanded, brooding over her. There was no warmth in his voice, and she missed that. She stopped, half off the bed, one foot on the floor. 'Stay in bed,' he insisted. 'For the rest of the day at least. Was it something you remembered?'

'No, I—I don't think so,' she sighed. It was getting harder and harder to maintain her cover-story. Harder and harder to stop herself from reaching out to him, confiding in him. And only her fears held her back.

Carefully she settled back in the bed, and once again he reached over gently and re-arranged the bottom of her *pareau*. The hard bitter look on his face gradually faded, to be replaced by—something. She was unable to put a name to it.

He started to say something to her, and then halted. Josie bounced into the room carrying a wicker tray. 'Breakfast—again,' the little girl announced with a giggle. 'I—could you sit up, and I could put the tray across your lap?'

He was around the bed before she could answer, piling pillows behind her, and then gently lifting her up to a sitting position. One of his arms accidentally brushed across her breasts. Tendrils of pleasure shot up into her mind. There was total recall of the night before. She caught her breath, then bit down hard on her lower lip to keep control. He hardly seemed to notice.

She managed a smile. Josie moved in close, and set the tray down across her lap with all the aplomb of a professional waiter. And then Miri was back, carrying a pot of fresh hot tea, and a puzzled look on her face. 'Tea is hot,' she offered, pouring a cup and setting the pot down on the bedside table. Rose flashed her a smile and picked up the cup in both hands, treasuring it as she sipped. Miri turned to Giles.

'He come back,' she said. 'We could talk outside, no?'

He followed her out into the hall. 'Who came back?'

'He came back,' the girl repeated. 'Almost impossible, no? He change his mind. The *tahu'a*.'

'Just like that? I thought he was going to have a fit when I mentioned the subject to him. What happened?'

'I don't know for truth. Is very involved. You know he would never answer a question from a *vahine*. He talk and talk and talk. Now, let me see I can get it right—he say, he receive a message from Tangora. Well, you know, he is an old man, and maybe not right in the head, *comprenez*.'

'Hey, all I know is that if he helps, everybody helps. And if he doesn't help, nobody helps. What message did he get?'

'He say Tangora say, "Help my daughter." That's all. So he comes to say he helps!'

'Good lord. I don't understand what's going on. Who the devil is Tangora?'

'The great sea-god. From the old religion. You know!'

'No, I guess I don't,' Giles sighed. 'I haven't had the time to meet all the old gods. Help my daughter?'

Miri waved a hand towards the bedroom. 'That is what Sam Apuka said. When he saw her in the— when—oh dear.' She giggled nervously, and tugged him away from the door and down the hall. Nervous giggles overtook her. She cupped her face in her hands and struggled to recover. 'Sam say when he first see her, the waves whisper something to him. *Ionei mea te Tamahine Tangora.* He swears he heard it. He tells it all over village. I think too much beer, big head. What you think?'

'What do I think? Lord, how can I think anything. What does that mean, what Sam said?'

'It mean, "Here is the daughter of the Sea-God." Sam swears all true. He go fishing with the *tahu'a* this morning, and he tell him. Crazy. Nobody b'lieve that kind of thing no more. All *haeire atu*—all that go away, long time ago. What you think?'

'Well it's beyond me' he sighed. 'But whatever, if he's willing to help, everything is set for next week. All we've got to do is keep Rose happy, and we're home safe. And in the meantime I've got to get some work done.'

They both walked slowly back into her bedroom. She was feasting daintily on a mango, laughing as Josie entertained her with tumbling exercises. The little girl stopped when he came in, and took his hand, tugging him towards the bed.

'With the ship coming next week,' he said, 'I've got

to get back to work. I promised to send in the next
three chapters by this boat, and agents are
devil-worshippers.'

'I'll look after Mommy,' Josie immediately volun-
teered.

'And I also,' Miri added. 'The kitchen work can wait.'

So there seemed to be nothing left for him to do. He
waved them all a half-salute and started for the door.

'Daddy!' Josie stamped her little foot. She sounded
considerably aggravated at him. Her head was jerking,
trying to convey a message.

'Oh!' A broad smile flashed across his face. He came
closer to the bed, leaned down, and caressed Rose's
forehead with his lips. Just a feather-touch. Her teacup
rattled in her hand, until finally she managed to get it
back to the tray. She folded her hands to hide the
shaking.

'Hen-pecked, that's what I am,' he complained
jovially as he left the room. Yes, and what does that
make me, Rose asked herself desperately. If I didn't
know for sure that he's trying to con me, I'd—well, I
don't know what I would do but I'd do something! If
he didn't scare me so much, I—oh damn!

Miri was busy clearing a place for a chair right next
to the bed. The Polynesian girl was laughing, flashing
her beautiful white teeth as if she knew what it was all
about. And I wish *I* did, Rose told herself. There's
something about Miri today, though, that—well, she
wasn't like this yesterday. I'll think what it is in a
minute. But right now there's Josie—and that awful
dress she's wearing. She looks as if she's being dressed
by the Abbot of a monastery, or something. My
daughter! I'll give her *my daughter* until it comes out
her ears. And his too.

'Josie? Why is that dress so short? Every time you
move I can see your underpants.'

'I—' the little girl had been caught unawares. 'I—all

my dresses are short,' she said defensively. 'My daddy likes them that way!'

'Then something must be done about it,' Rose said determinedly. 'What you need is some shorts, and a few blouses. Easy things to make. Do we have a sewing machine in the house?'

'*Ea*' Miri tendered. 'Yes. An old Singer pedal machine. You know to make such a machine go?'

'You bet,' she responded agressively. 'Among other things. Or you could wear a *pareau*, Josie?'

'My Daddy won't let me,' the girl sighed. 'He says I'm not to run around naked like the other kids. I'm supposed to be somebody. I don't know who.'

'My husband's a snob,' Rose chuckled. 'And I didn't know.'

'But you know so very little,' Miri giggled. 'Except sewing machines. That you remember! Some things come back, no? First croissants, and now sewing machines.'

'I—ah—well, I didn't really remember.' Rose struggled to cover the mistake. 'It just *seems* that I think of sewing machines as something that——' Oh lord, shut up, she told herself, the more you fumble around, the worse it gets! And there's a policeman coming next week. To get you, Rosie Lambert, what else. I wonder if he'll have a picture of me on a 'wanted' poster? Rose Lambert, jailbird! Come on, Rose, there's no use glooming about it. When he gets here, that'll be a different story. In the meantime, live!

'And until I'm able to throw a thing or two together, Josie,' she continued, 'you'll put away all that nonsense, and wear a *pareau*. Miri, could you find something?'

'Plenty *pareaux*,' the Polynesian woman cautioned, 'but the girl is right. Mr Gendron, he will, how you say, blow the stack off?'

'Not to worry,' Rosa chuckled. 'I'm the mother, no?'

She added the little ending in bravado. Okay, let him rant and rave. If he's invented a mother for his child, he'll have to put up with her strong character and firm ideas—or he'll blow the works on whatever scheme it is that *he*'s working on!

Josie was laughing hysterically, rocking back and forth on her heels. Look at that, Rose told herself. Even the kid knows what's going on, and me, I don't know from beans. 'You don't like the idea?' she asked.

'Oh, I love it. I really do.' There were tears running down the little cheeks. Happy tears. Her feelings were too much for her battered French, so the child switched over to English. 'We haven't had so much fun in years, and I like it a lot,' she teased. 'Only you gotta train Daddy better. Oh I'm so glad you came—I—I mean, it's wonderful to have my mother back again!' A clock chimed in the hall. Ten o'clock. I think I've put in a six-teen hour day already, and it's only ten in the morning, Rose sighed to herself.

'I gotta go. I hafta study for two hours every morning,' the little girl said. Her eyes pleaded for a day off, but Rose was not about to fall into *that* trap so early in the game.

'Then get on with it,' she commanded gently. 'And be sure to bring your papers in here this afternoon so I can check them.'

She earned a smile—a broad happy smile—and the child ran for the door.

'She never walks anywhere?' Miri turned back to her at the question. 'Every time I've seen her she's always running,' Rose explained.

'All children the same,' the Polynesian returned. 'Childhood filled with many joys. If she walks slow, she will miss something. I go find her two, three *pareaux*.'

'Come back afterwards,' Rose pleaded. 'I need to talk to *someone*. I feel as if I were on a merry-go-round that keeps going faster at each turn.'

'Merry-go-round? *Me fifi roa*. I don't understand?'

'Forget it.' She waved a thank you hand. 'Hurry back. You can put off some of the work, can't you?'

Miri looked at her with her soul in her eyes, lovingly. 'In the islands there is always time for people,' she said softly. 'You rest. I come at once, no?'

She was as good as her word. Not ten minutes later she moved gracefully through the doorway with a second pot of tea. 'I can use that,' Rose laughed, wishing that she knew the secret of that graceful walk. 'Now. Set a spell, as they say back home in my country. And tell me something. Anything. You and Mr Apuka?'

The other woman smiled at her as she settled into the chair. 'You read faces, no? Yes. Me and Sam. We are friends for years, when I am a child. Then he goes away five years, you know. That is the island sadness. All the young men, they want work. They go away and work for the CEP, for the Fisheries, for anybody. And then when they finish they like too much the cities, and the entertainment. They go Tahiti, live around Papeete. Think it is the best life, you know—and they never come back. But Sam, he comes back. And last night he knows I am child no longer, and we think as before, you understand, so I move my mat to his house. And maybe, when the Priest comes by on the supply boat—oh, not next week, the one after that—maybe we get married. That part is not so important, you understand.'

'I'm not sure that I do,' Rose laughed. 'But it's what *you* think that's important. I read Margaret Meade's book about Samoa, of course.'

'Ah see!' Miri chortled. 'You remember more! Too bad not something else. I know about Margaret Meade. I go to school in Bora Bora, and we study. Her book is nice for *popa'a*, but——'

'But?'

'But not exactly true. One thing she does not

understand. Our people wish to make their friends happy, so we tell them what they want to hear. Happens all the time. Suppose we go walk, you and me, and we see a bird. You say, look, is *Nono Anu* bird. I look. Is not *Nono Anu*, is *Ute Ute Anu*. But you want it to be *Nono Anu*—and to say you are wrong makes you unhappy. Bird, he don't care what to call him. Me, I don't care what to call him so long he don't eat me. So I say, oh yes, is *Nono Anu*. You understand?'

'I suppose I do,' Rose returned. 'But it's confusing to a stranger. You'll have to put up with my ignorance for a while, I'm afraid.'

'You no stranger,' Miri said seriously. 'You *Te Tamahine*. That's plenty. You one of us.'

'I wish I could be,' Rose sighed. 'You are all so free. I wish I could be that way. I wish I could even wear a *pareau* the way you do. But I don't have the nerve. You are so free.'

'Hah!' Miri laughed so hard the tears welled. 'We not free, not at all. You look, but do not see. We live by custom. Everything has custom. We say the old ways are gone, but on the small islands they are still here, hiding behind mask, no? The old *tapuus* still run. What happens to *vahine* who stays to watch the men swim? Pele comes out of her mountain, that's what, and punish that fool. You better b'lieve it. And you better not wear *pareau* like I do.'

'Well why not, for goodness sakes?'

'Because, what you think—you get all over sunburn. Then you no good for your man at all, huh? I do something like that myself, Sam, he gives me a good knock, no?'

'Okay, I give up,' Rose giggled. 'So find me some cloth, and I'll make Josie and I both some skirts and some blouses.'

'I bring the machine this afternoon,' Miri promised. 'Now, what else you want to talk about?'

I want to talk about *him*, Rose told herself desperately. My—my husband. 'How long has Mr Gendron—how long have we been here on the island,' she asked cautiously, not knowing whether Miri was a part of the conspiracy or not.

'Oh——' the island girl was fumbling for words. Rose's heart sank. Not another one, she prayed desperately. 'The child—you know—she is born here on *Te Tuahine*, but I am not here at that time. And then he come back three years ago? Yes, three years. He is a friend of Mr Maravais, the man who builds this Big House. He buys everything, that Giles. Whole island belongs to him now. And he writes. Locks door in study, hang red sign in hall. Only room in house with a door. He says to me, he says—Hey, Miri, you tell all *kanaka* boy anybody comes to my room when red sign hangs out, gets plenty trouble, b'lieve me. So then he stays six months, and then he goes off. We don't see him for long time. But then when he comes, he brings child.'

'Just the child?'

'*Aue*, now. What have I said. No, no. He brings you and the child.'

'Two years ago?'

'Pretty close. We measure time better by supply boats coming, not by years.'

And that makes one more, Rose thought sadly. They're all in it. Everybody in the house! Two years ago Papa and I were living high on the hog in Monaco. That was one of our good years. The last one, come to think of it. But—come on, Rosie. Why let it get you down? Pull up your socks and get things moving. That's what Papa always said. You've been just a little loose with the truth yourself, haven't you dearie? Papa. Where can he be? I know he's not dead. I can still feel that bond between us. He's not dead—he's just—somewhere else. And now? Giles has some plan, some programme. And he needs me for a wife. Complete with a long background and history. So I just can't be Rose Lambert, can I? When the policeman comes, if he doesn't have a picture, why here I'll be. Mrs Giles Gendron, complete with husband and child, all who've known me since Caesar was a pup! All I've got to do is keep my cool and agree with everything they tell me. Well, most everything. And there's only a week to wait.

'Thank you, Miri,' she sighed. 'I feel—just a little bit tired. I'd like to rest for a while. Do you mind?'

It was true. Her eyes were heavy. And the weak smile she mustered was enough to convince the native girl. Miri watched the eyelids slowly drop, heard the sigh of relaxation as all the limbs fell loose. '*Iorana oe*,' she whispered over the sleeping blonde beauty, and flowed gracefully out of the room.

Rose slept through the lunch, and through the silent afternoon, when even the birds seemed to take the time to rest. He came with the child to look in from the doorway, but nothing disturbed her deep and quiet sleep. No nightmares, no memories, no pains. To all intents her brain was turned off, and her body relaxed in a jumble of loose limbs that brought a smile to his face. He came back twice during the afternoon and night. Once he re-arranged her *pareau*, smoothing it down over her lovely legs. The second time he brought a damp cloth and wiped away the beads of perspiration from her forehead. She noticed neither appearance, nor noted the length of time he stood by the bed brooding over her, a strangely warm smile on his face. The night passed, and it was morning again.

CHAPTER FOUR

SHE lay on the beach in the late afternoon and stretched, squirming against the soft whiteness of the sand like a cat. The little teddy which she had sewn up for herself in place of a bathing suit, was just enough cloth to be decent as long as it was dry. Wet, it was of no more use as a cover than a fistful of cobwebs. Her wrap-around skirt, brought along to meet the Polynesian requirements for modesty, was rolled up under her head as a pillow.

She suppressed a giggle as she looked down at her *daughter*, beside her. Here they were, two *popa'a*, dressed mother-and-daughter style in the same cut and colour of outfit, the result of the several long hours Rose had spent over the ancient sewing machine. Out of the thousands of bolts of *pareau*-cloth on the island, and there seemed to be at least twenty miles of the stuff, she had concocted for them both several sets of wrap-around skirts and sleeveless blouses, and a round half-dozen of the head-to-toe Missionary dresses, the *muumuu*. Not exactly high fashion, to be sure, but the best her needle could provide. There had been no help from the island women. They all looked at it as an exercise in foolishness. Pleasant foolishness, but . . .

'Now, if I only had some decent underwear,' she sighed.

'You mean like silk and lace and all that stuff?' Josie giggled.

'Like silk and lace,' she returned, pushing up the brim of her big straw hat to get a better look. They had established a close rapport, she and this little girl who claimed to be her daughter. And perhaps more than a rapport, perhaps more than just a liking. Which may be only over-compensation, Rose warned herself. To make up for the fact that that father of hers scares me to death! Every time I look around quickly, there he is, staring at me. As if I were the next dish to be served!

She settled back again, hands clasped behind her head, hat pulled forward to shade her face. At that angle only the narrow line of surf smashing at the reef was within her sights. The whole world seemed to be at peace. And look at me! It was, what—Monday night when I came ashore. I don't remember Tuesday at all. Wednesday I met both the Gendrons, and came down with amnesia. Thursday he told me they were my 'family'. Friday I seemed to have slept through a day, somewhere. Saturday we walked around and kept out of each other's way. He and I, I mean. Sunday I went to the church service. Sam Apuka led the service. I didn't understand a word of what he was saying—but wasn't the singing marvellous? It almost seemed spontaneous, interrupting the homily when the spirit moved, first one voice, then a dozen, then the entire congregation. And what could have a nicer sound than '*Rock of Ages*' sung to a hula beat!

Monday. What did I do on Monday. I sewed, mostly. The *tahu'a* came by and we had one of those conversations where he went away happily, and I hadn't the slightest idea what he was talking about. And here it is Tuesday. The ship comes tomorrow. Or should I say the police come tomorrow. Looking for Rose Lambert, of course. Which gives me just twenty-four hours to practise up on being Rose Gendron, wife, mother—and Lord help me, what else? Lover? I haven't done too well in that line so far—and I've got to do better! 'You hear me, Rose?'

'What did you say?' Josie was up on one elbow, staring at her. Her tiny body glittered from the applications of coconut oil her father had insisted on.

'Nothing. I was talking to myself. I find it very

important to see if I agree with myself!' The little girl's eyes sparkled at her, proof that the affection was not all one-sided. And then, because Rose's mind was squirreling around with her own million problems, it slipped. 'Didn't your other mother ever do that?'

'She didn't make no funny—ohhhh!' The little hands went up to cover her mouth, and a look of astonished reproach swept over the elfin face. The eyes turned stormy. 'You made me say that! You made me!' The child jumped to her feet, indignation showing in every angle of her body. Indignation, and something else. Fear? Rose struggled to sitting position, an apology on the tip of her tongue. But by that time the girl was already several yards down the beach, running and crying at the same time.

Now you've damn well done it, she scolded herself as she let her muscles relax and collapsed back on to the sand. Now you've really blown the whole thing! What kind of a stupid amnesiac are you, Rose Lambert? Do you have some sort of death wish or something? The day before the boat is due in, the one with the cop on board, you have to shoot off your mouth and blow everything! And now the poor little kid will run to her dear daddy. God, I wonder what *he'll* do! Wearily, disgusted with herself, she readjusted the straw hat over her face and closed her eyes. There really wasn't anything else to do. Was there, Rose? No place to run, is there?

No place to run. No place to—what was it he had said. 'Nobody ever goes up there. If it has a name, only the *tahu'a* knows what it is. Everybody else just pretends that there's no mountain up there.' Pele's mountain! Her eyes snapped open. What about that! If the police were coming on the supply boat, you could presume they would have to leave with that same boat. How else? So all I have to do, she reasoned, is to sit tight, pretend I'm a loving wife, and then as soon as word comes about the boat, I disappear up into the mountain that isn't there! I'll need food—no, I guess I won't. There are plenty of orange and breadfruit trees and—oh Lord, everything up there. And plenty of water. All I have to do is go, right? C'mon, girl!

She hustled herself to her feet, picked up her odds and ends, and started back towards the house. It was a long walk. For some reason the two of them had ventured all the way down the bay to a point that looked out into the ocean, just under the peak of Mona Aui. She had been attracted by the colour. Down here just a few feet from where they had stopped, the sand was all black, a reminder of the island's volcanic past.

Across from her somewhere in the village, she could hear the soft sound of Polynesian music as a group of ukeleles strummed, and a slack-string guitar picked out one of the haunting island melodies. The music wandered across the water just as the first of the outrigger canoes moved in to the bay from the lagoon, with the day's catch. Each note seemed to fall out of the air fully-rounded, like some perfectly shaped rain drop. She smiled at her own romanticism, shook her hair to free it of the loose sand, and hurried up the stairs to the Big House.

'Hi!' He was standing on the veranda as she made it up the last of the stairs, head down. Now's the time, she told herself. Pour it on. You catch flies with honey, not with vinegar!

'Hi yourself.' She put a smile into the phrase, walked directly to him, and gave him an enthusiastic hug. He was so startled that for a moment he had trouble juggling the drink he held in his hand. And then he reacted. His free hand came around her shoulders, pressing her into his chest gently but firmly. She turned her head aside to lay her cheek against him.

The hair on his chest was a light brown, almost the colour of his well-tanned skin. Soft, not wiry as she had expected. For just a moment she overcame her fears, her tensions, and relaxed against him. She could hear and feel the soft bubble of laughter that ran up from his lungs. Mr and Mrs Giles Gendron, she mused. The whole thing seemed so startlingly real. She squeezed herself against him, then whirled away, accepting the drink he offered. It was something and scotch. Tall, cool, refreshing. She sipped avidly at it, then accepted the hand he offered. He towed her around to the side of the house, where several lounge chairs waited. She sank into one of them, breathing a huge sigh of relief.

'Busy day?' He toasted her with his glass.

'Mm,' she answered. 'Yes and no. We walked too far. All the way down to the black sand.' She gestured in the general direction of Mona Aui.

'Josie came home all upset,' he stated. And if you're waiting for me to explain it will be a mighty cold day on *Te Tuahine*, she promised under her breath.

'Did you ask her why?'

'No,' he admitted. 'She ducked out of the way. That kid is getting to be a typical woman. I like the bathing suits you made. And the outfits. I just hate to see my only daughter grow up like a native kid.'

'I'm married to a snob?'

'No,' he protested, and then slightly crestfallen, 'Well, maybe yes. Is that wrong?'

'I don't know,' she sighed. 'I just don't remember whether I think that's bad or good.'

'You still don't remember a thing?'

'Nothing.' And then she had another thought. Maybe I shouldn't make it all that easy for him. There's some reason why he doesn't want me to remember. Maybe if I turn the screw, I might get him to tell me what's going on. 'I keep having this dream,' she said softly. 'I keep dreaming that I'm in a life raft, and it's pitching and tossing—and that's all.'

'That's all you remember?'

'About the dream? Yes, that's all.' Keep your voice low, she commanded herself. Be a little bemused. 'Yes,' she repeated, savouring the words, 'that's all. Just the life raft.'

'Something subconcious,' he offered, taking another pull at his glass. 'You saw the little raft down on the beach and it was so out of the ordinary that you remembered it.'

Thank you, Dr Freud, she muttered under her breath. The opportunity to give him another dig was too good to be passed up. 'Maybe I should tell the Inspector about it when he arrives tomorrow?'

'Oh, I wouldn't do that!' He almost dropped his glass in his hurry to reassure her. 'A dream like that has nothing of interest to the police. No, certainly don't bother him with something like that!'

'Well—all right.' She could taste the excitement. It was like baiting a bear. Half the thrill came from knowing that he could unpredictably strike back. But he owes me one more shot, she promised herself. At her demure best she looked him straight in the eye. 'But won't he ask where the liferaft came from? It's so unusual.'

'Not all that unusual,' he returned. 'Besides, the Inspector will be late getting in tomorrow, and I doubt if he'll notice a little thing like a liferaft. You seem different tonight.'

'Different?'

'I don't know if that's the exact word, but you're more relaxed. Almost as if you had—accepted the situation.'

'Accepted? That's a strange word to use.'

'I—yes,' he stammered. 'Perhaps I should have said becoming more adjusted to things. I'm not very clever with words.'

'But you make your living—our living—with words!'

'Ah, but that's different. There are two different languages, you know. The written one and the spoken one. And besides, when I'm at work my characters do exactly what I tell them, and never never ever talk back.'

'Hardly ever?' His eyes flashed at her as she ducked her head in disgust. If you plan to make this situation last, Rose Lambert, she lectured herself, you'll have to stop quoting Gilbert and Sullivan. This man is no dunce. Hardly ever, indeed! Fool! Divert him, quickly. Fight. Argue! 'Is that what Josie and I are supposed to do,' she asked sweetly. 'Never talk back and do exactly what we're told?'

'More or less.' He was laughing at her, those big dark eyes sparkling out a challenge—one she dare not accept. She gulped the rest of her drink, folded her hands demurely in her lap, and leaned back against the softness of the chair. That predatory look was forming around the edges of his mouth. His lips were slightly parted, showing magnificent teeth. Lord, I've got to get away from him! She found herself shivering. She brushed her hair forward around her face, stood up out of the lounge chair, and mumbled at him. 'I've got to check up on Josie.' She was gone before his 'what did you say,' caught up with her.

The child was not in the house. Following the twinge of her intuition, she slipped her feet into a pair of rubber thong slippers, and went down the hill to the fresh-water pool behind the dam. She could hear the sound of argument as she came closer, but only the child was there when finally Rose wove her way through the stands of bamboo and out on to the banked edge of the pool.

'Josie?' The girl had seen her, but turned her back defiantly, pretending to be watching something up near the caved in top of Pele's mountain. Rose hesitated for a moment, and then walked over and dropped a hand on the child's shoulder. 'Josie,' she repeated, doing her best to keep her voice at a soft persuasive pitch. 'I'm sorry if I made you feel bad. I would never do that intentionally. Please?'

The child wheeled around and grabbed at her as if she were the last refuge in the world. The tears began just as her little head buried itself between Rose's breasts. 'I *want* you to be my mother,' the child sobbed. 'I *want* you—for always!'

Rose caressed the silky blonde hair, made soothing noises, held the slender body close. 'Forever's a long long time,' she sighed.

'But that's what I want,' Josie sobbed. 'You're—nice. So very nice. You do nice things, and you say nice things, and it's fun to be with you, and you're so—so soft and I like to cuddle up with you, and—and I can trust you, that's what. You don't make kid-talk at me, and—well—I just need you to be my mother!'

'But I *am* your mother, Josie. At least that's what your daddy said.'

The tears slowed, came to a stop, and were properly terminated by a couple of wild sniffs. 'You know that's not true, don't you,' the little girl accused.

Once again the whirlwind rattled through Rose's brain. You know that's not true! Of course you know. But there's a world of difference between knowing something secretly in your heart, and coming out plain and outspoken with it. I *need* you to be my mother? How many times had Rose herself wanted to say something like that to the multitude of women her father had brought home after her mother died. I *need* you! That was the operative word. And I can trust you, that's what!

Her hand automatically stroked the girl's glistening hair. 'Yes, I knew that,' she answered softly. 'I don't know why your daddy said what he did. I knew it wasn't true, but he must have had some reason for saying so. But all that isn't important. Not any more. We start from today, shall we? If you really need me, Josie, I'll be your mother for as long and as well as I'm able. I can't make any promises about being a wonderful mother, you understand, because I don't have any mothering practice. And I can't promise it will last forever, because only God knows what's around the corner for either of us. But I *will* try, if that's what you want.'

The hug became ecstasy. 'It is. That's just what I want—Mommy. Oh, I love you so!' And because that was an expression she hadn't heard a great deal of lately, Rose Lambert had difficulty stifling the tears that threatened to break loose. They strolled back up to the house, arm in arm, the girl's chatter bouncing off the close-knit growth that hemmed the path, frightening a flamboyant big-billed toucan who was busy building in the bush. So much so that the bird haunted them the rest of the way up the path, screaming raucous insults at them as only a toucan can.

'Don't mention this to your father,' Rose prompted, as they stopped at the foot of the stairs. 'He might not quite understand. Just between us girls?' Josie looked a trifle doubtful, and then gave in.

'You betcha! *Oui! Ea!*' And having been reassured in all three languages, the pair of them tumbled up the stairs to answer the call of the dinner bell that hung next to the hibachi charcoal grates in the kitchen.

Dinner was a lovely meal. He had managed to squeeze in a whole chapter of the new book, and it was running well. To be honest about it, it was running away from him. None of the characters were following the plot line. He found it hard not to laugh when he met Rose's eye over the steamed Bonito, the fried breadfruit, the sweet pau-paus. And my characters never talk back? Lord, how pompous can you get. Look at her sitting there in the long *muumuu* she had made for herself. The missionaries had designed the gown so that every woman looked like a sack. Rose looked like a million dollars. Of course it wasn't black, the colour the women wore on Moorea. How could it be when there was only the brilliant *pareau* cloth to work with! Magnificent. Her pale oval face was accumulating a tan, just the right colour-contrast to set off her hair. And those deep green eyes, like a cat, always watching! She laughed at one of Josie's little jokes. All of her laughed, and the *muumuu* clung close to her exciting breasts, and shook with glee. He could hardly unpin his eyes. He had completely lost track of the conversation.

'Toucans?' he asked, when prodded.

'Yes. We saw a whole flight of them. How in the world did they get here?'

'You mean how did a short-range South American bird arrive here in the Pacific islands?' So I'm stalling, he told himself. How else am I going to make some sense out of what's going on. Look at the two of them. They really *could* be mother and daughter. 'Well, I'm not an ornithologist,' he commented. 'All I really know is what I've heard from Sam and the *tahu'a*. When he's talking to me, that is. The long range birds like the frigate—I don't know where they came from originally, but they're on most of the islands. They can navigate at will, over great distances. And the herring gulls. They island-hop. The plover is a migratory bird. You only see them here at certain times, when they get ready to enter the Pacific fly-ways. About the long-tailed cuckoo, I haven't any idea. They're just here. And please don't ask me how any of them find directions.'

'Like the navigators in the great canoes, Daddy?'

'Well, no, not exactly, love. And all the great canoes are gone. I doubt if anyone in the Society Islands today knows how to make a great canoe. I read an article once about a man in Samoa who conducts schools, and builds canoes. But he's the only one left, I'm afraid. No, men navigated a little differently than the birds. They used the stars, the wind, water patterns, birds in flight, clouds, anything. You know that all the big islands have a cloud that hangs over them? We have one, Tahiti has one—all the islands. Distinctive clouds that you can see for miles at sea. And of course Sirius rises and sets exactly on the latitude of Tahiti. So if you sail at night, and want to go to Tahiti, you only need to keep Sirius directly overhead. Next question?'

'Well, you didn't answer the first one,' Rose commented. 'About the toucans? Or does that long speech indicate that you don't know about toucans? They came in the war canoes, perhaps?'

'Don't be a wiseacre,' he laughed. 'Toucans are the easiest answer in the world. Like a great deal of the life on these islands, the Toucans were brought in by man. To be specific, Sam Apuka's father brought six pairs of them in from South America not more than twenty years ago. Their only enemies are palm-rats and kids who want them as pets. Any other questions, children?'

She kicked his ankle under the table. It seemed the sort of thing any self-respecting wife would do in the face of such blatant chauvinism. It hurt her toe more than it did his ankle. Miri, bringing in a bowl of fruit for dessert, tch-tched when she saw the action. Polynesian girls never strike their men—even when they need it!

Josie needed no coaxing to get her to bed. It had been a hard day indeed for the little girl. She clutched at Rose's fingers while her father read her a bedtime story, one of the scarey kind that she really liked, from an inexhaustible book. At least it seemed to have no end, this magic book. It also had several pages missing. And sometimes he held it upside down as he read. But the same story was never heard twice, and no one else could ever find the right page and a favourite story, no matter how hard they tried. Unless it could be that his fertile imagination was making them all up as he went along? At least Josie accused him of doing so, and he felt the need to make a blanket denial.

He always judged the story-endings to a nicety, waiting until the child's eyes began to blink before the tale roared into some drastic and logical climax. And then he would close the book and watch as his daughter slipped over the reef into slumberland.

He could feel the stirring of a breeze on the back of his neck as he completed the tale. Just enough to flutter the small hairs, nothing more. It came loaded with the base odour of burning charcoal, the sharp ginger smell of the frangipani, the penetrating sharpness of vanilla. Both of his women seemed to be dreaming. Josie, her eyes completely shut, cuddled on her right side facing her mother—Lord, how easy it is to think that way—her mother. Rose, leaning back against the bamboo chair, her eyes half-closed, a smile playing at the corners of her mouth. She was still holding the baby's hand.

He felt that stirring within him again. Not just lust, playing at his loins, but something—something more. Some faint regret, some remorse. If only we had met ten years ago! But that couldn't be, his practical mind told him. Ten years ago she must have been a child, hardly Josie's age. Is that what's wrong with me? Middle-age regrets? Crying out to youth to be sustained? But his romantic mind was not willing to give up the dream. Hell, the girl is—what—twenty? To my thirty-five? What's wrong with that? After I get free of all this mess, we'll—The child stirred, breaking his chain of thought. Rose gently disengaged her hand and stood up. He followed her out of the room, around the house to the open veranda where talk would not disturb the sleeper.

'Another drink?' he offered.

'Yes, but no alcohol,' she decided. He helped her into one of the lounge chairs and went over to the table where drinkables were kept. 'Orange juice?'

'Yes, that's fine.'

He poured her a tall cool glass from the evaporative cooler, then fixed himself a double shot of Scotch. After serving her, he carried his small glass over to the edge of the veranda and looked up. High above him the scattered stars wheeled in train, the Southern Cross high in the sky. A three-quarter moon trailed fingers of silver across the tiny waves running beyond the reef. The roar of the sovereign sea played counterpoint to all the other noises of the night.

He came back to her chair. The roof of the veranda kept her face in a half-light. He felt the urge to reach down, to tilt her chin up into the moonlight, to—but he fought off the urge. It was always there, damn it. The need to touch her! Damn! He squeezed his glass and tossed off the remainder of its contents.

'You know a lot about the islands, don't you,' she queried softly. Even her voice gave him a strange sensation. It was a soft husky contralto that climbed up to a squeak when she was excited.

'Some,' he returned. 'I've always had this thing about the South Seas. Read everything I could when I was a kid. I came out here for two years—two *wanderjahren*—after I finished at Ohio State. The university, not the prison.'

'I never thought otherwise,' she giggled. 'You're altogether too—too slippery—to get penned up in the pen.' The moment the words were out she regretted them. Poor choice—slippery!

He turned away from her to cover his surprise. A beautiful nature, a magnificent body, and a tongue as sharp as a rapier. Well, if you let a word or two turn you off, you deserve everything you get, he lectured himself. And went back to the topic at hand.

'So I and a couple of my friends put together all our money and bought a schooner, and went into the copra trade. Two years it took us, to go broke and to discover that there were a million ways to live better than hauling copra. But we got a good education out of it, and my first book was based on my experiences. And you?' He threw the question in as a teaser, and got back the answer he deserved.

'Who me? As far as I know I've never been in the copra trade, nor sailed a schooner anywhere. Although I suppose I must have read my share of South Sea island romances. I'm sorry, Giles, but I still just don't remember. I really try—but I don't remember. Was that recently when you did all that?'

'Ah—no.' He was caught short by her smooth transition to another subject. 'No, that was some years ago. Back when I was your age.' He had finally manoeuvered her into the moonlight, and now he searched her face for a response or a rejection. For any sign at all, to tell the truth. 'I'm thirty-five, you know.'

'Do I know,' she asked hesitantly. 'I—that really doesn't seem to be very old to me. I'm only—lord, I don't even know how old I am. But thirty-five isn't very old—at least I don't think so!'

And then she was back in the shadows, and he hadn't seen a single sign for or against. Just the words. But they were enough to go on. Thirty-five isn't very old—and by Harry I feel younger already. It's almost as if she just stamped a visa on my passport; a permit to enter youth again!

Now then, the aircraft will land at Maupiti about noontime with the packages and the policeman. The supply boat will sail almost immediately. It will take them six hours to get here, at flank speed. Which is just as the tide is making. The best time in the world to come through the reef. If only I can keep her sweet until then!

And that's what is confusing all my thinking. I don't dare to trust my emotions. What I feel for her has to be balanced against what I feel about her. She's the queenpin of my little play. The play either works, or Josie and I go down the drain. But if it *does* work—I swear it, Rose whoever you are, I'll devote all my energy and all my time and all my money—if it comes to that—to find out what *your* problem is. To find out just what it is that you're so busy forgetting!

'You're very quiet,' she probed.

'Just thinking. There's a dance over at the village tonight. Care to walk down that way?'

'A *tamure?*'

'Where in the world did you learn that word?'

'I—I don't know. It just came to me. Will it be a *tamure?*'

'No, no—nothing like that. Just a little get-together. The *tamure* is only for some big celebration, and it's a wild time, lady. A lot of tourists come looking as if they expect a Hawaiian hula. Huh! They go away with red faces every time. The *tamure* is wild—but wild. It's a real fertility dance. And if that's what they were having, I wouldn't have invited you to go!'

'Well,' she giggled. 'I learn something new about you every day. First, you admit to being a snob, and now it's obvious you're some sort of prude to boot!'

It was all true, but it hurt to hear her say so. He turned away again, staring down the bay to where a bonfire had just been lit. And I'm learning something about me every day too, he told himself cynically. Things I never knew before. Is this why Helen and I couldn't stay married? It startled him when Rose ghosted up beside him, leaned a shapely thigh against his, and put her small hand on his bare arm. 'I didn't mean to upset you,' she offered contritely.

Instantly that spark was back. Not just the words, but the touch, the warmth of her, and the sweet smell. There was no perfume on the island, save that of the flowers, no soaps save what the islanders made from the coconut. Nevertheless she smelled—enticing, sexy, earthy, clean, honest—all the words fitted.

'It's not important,' he gruffed, finding it necessary to clear his throat. 'Would you like to go down?'

'I don't think so,' she sighed. No matter what he said, the words had a coolness about them which had not been there before. 'Couldn't we just sit and talk?'

'If you like.' He guided her back to the lounge chairs, pulled two of them close together. He helped her re-settle herself before he dropped down on to the adjacent chair.

After a moment of silence, she asked, 'The boat comes tomorrow?'

'Yes. Late tomorrow afternoon. Around six or seven perhaps, depending on the weather.'

'It will be a big event, I suppose?'

'Hey, considering that it only comes four times a year, yes, I guess you could call it a big event. We re-stock our staples, get in a few luxuries.'

'I never see anybody working. What do they use for money?'

'Copra,' he laughed. 'Always the copra. They could get rich from it if it didn't smell so bad. The entire village has managed to put together—oh, five tons of copra since the last ship came. They'll load that up, haggle about it until dawn, and then not stir another finger until close to the next boat time.'

'And then?'

'It depends on what they think they need. If they want a great deal, things will hum around here. If not, they'll make a stab at it, and quit.'

'Is it hard, making copra?'

He reached over and picked up her hand. 'Why you really don't know anything, do you! Copra is dried coconut. They take it over behind Mount Atau to avoid the smell, crack the nuts, and leave it in the sun to dry.'

'You sound as if you don't quite approve.'

'That's not true, Rose. It's their way of life, out here on the outer islands. In Tahiti they all live by the clock, punch time cards, obey traffic lights. Out here they live as they want to. No, I approve all right. Not everybody in the world should be stuck with their noses to grindstones. To tell the truth, maybe I'm sorry for myself, not for them. They live the good life, and I envy them. Even if my Calvinist upbringing won't allow me to emulate them.'

She changed the subject. 'There's a shooting star. Do you make a wish?'

'Silly. You only wish on the "first star I see tonight." And I already did that.'

'Really? What did you wish for?'

'Oh no, lady. If I tell, I don't get my wish.'

'Then how in the world can anyone know if you got your wish?'

'Easy,' he whispered. He leaned over her chair, trapping her within his arms, pulling her over towards him. He was prepared for a struggle, and wrath to follow, but nothing happened. She seemed almost to flow across the space between them, a frictionless being, and suddenly he could feel the soft moist warmth of her lips under his as he gently kissed her. He had been planning this for the past three hours. Planning for the moment when he would offer her just a touch—the tiniest touch—of himself.

But as soon as the contact was made, all his plans went up in smoke. There was that spark again, that static spark that seemed to leap between them, crackling as it struck where their lips were joined. And it seemed to affect her as well as himself. Instead of struggling against him, she squirmed closer, arms threading themselves around his neck, pulling him closer into the trap that was her soft body.

He went willingly, all sense of proportion lost in the dazzling feeling that blinded, deafened, and turned him into a raw pulsing mass of emotion. He pressed harder, until her lips opened to him, inviting his penetration.

His hands swarmed up and down her back, up and down her sides, defeated by the folds of the capacious *muumuu*, but still relishing the softness, the warmth. She was moaning in his ear, moaning something he could not quite understand. And then suddenly she stiffened in his arms, and the contact was broken.

In a fragment of a second her hands came down to his chest, beating on him, forcing him away. He tried to recapture the warmth by holding on. Her hands beat a tattoo against his chest, against his cheeks, but to no avail. And then she began to shiver. He felt it instantly. All up and down her spine she was shaking. Something wet fell on to his bare chest. Something salty wet. He continued to search for what they had lost, but there was no hope of finding it. She was sobbing now, tearing sobs that wracked her frame. He took two deep breaths to settle himself, and then slowly pushed her away, keeping control of her by hands which clutched her shoulders.

'What is it?' he whispered. 'What?'

'I'm afraid,' she sobbed, almost collapsing in his hands.

'Afraid of me?' He had never even *thought* the idea before, never mind voiced it. A woman who is afraid of me? What sort of monster does she think I am, for God's sake! What kind—and yet there she is, shaking and shivering as if I were Gargantua, and she the virgin in my clutches. My God! Deep inside his stomach revolted, forcing bile up into his throat as his hands shook slightly, and released her. She fell back on to the chair, still sobbing. He struggled to his feet, looked down at her huddled form, and then around the horizon as if to see if he were still grounded in reality.

'Well, I certainly didn't mean to frighten you,' he growled bitterly. He was trying to hide his damaged male ego, and not quite succeeding. 'I didn't realise that I was that much poison. Good night!'

He stormed down off the veranda and plunged on to

the trail that led to the beach. She sat up and swung her legs off the lounger, trying to stem the flow of tears with her knuckles. He was outlined against the lights across the way as he started down the stairs to the beach. Gradually he sank below the level of the top step, and was out of sight.

She forced herself to her feet and went over to the edge of the veranda, resting against one of the bamboo pillars that supported the roof. The tears slowed, and finally stopped.

'And now look what you've done, Rosie Lambert,' she sighed. 'Call him back? No, don't. Things are bad enough as they are. Let it go—until after the police have left. And then, if everything works out and I don't get arrested, then I'll tell him. Tell him that it's me I'm scared of, not him. I've never felt this way before. Never! Lord knows what I would have let him do tonight—what I would have helped him do—if it had gone on for another two minutes!'

'Mommy? A sleepy figure in a long flowing nightgown peered around the doorjamb and came out into the moonlight. 'I thought I heard you crying. Were you crying?'

'Yes, love.' She held out a hand and the child came up to be enveloped in a hug.

'And you were talking to yourself. That's a bad sign.'

'So you say.' She tickled under the little chin, just enough to bring a giggle. 'Mothers talk to themselves all the time, didn't you know that? It's a lot easier than trying to cxplain to Daddys what life is all about. Back to bed, ragamuffin. Scoot!'

CHAPTER FIVE

THE ship came up to the reef at six o'clock, almost an hour before sunset, when the tide was almost at its highest. They watched it from the veranda, Giles, Josie, and herself. The little girl was on pins and needles, anxious to go. Most of the villagers had already headed for the rickety dock near the mouth of Pakuo Bay, where the sloping shoulder of Mona Atau provided protection from the trade winds.

'There's no hurry,' he said. 'Relax. And for goodness sakes, finish your dinner.' There was a snap in his voice. She had never heard him speak to his daughter like that before. 'They still have their boats out,' he added.

'What in the world are they doing?' Rose wanted to appear uninterested, but couldn't. The ancient freighter had come to a halt, and two small boats were out ahead of it, doing something over the narrow entrance to the reef.

'They're sounding the channel,' he told her grimly. 'It's an artificial channel, you remember ... Oh Lord, I'm sorry. I didn't mean that. The channel was blasted out of the reef about twenty years ago. Before that time this harbour just wasn't accessible.'

'So what has that to do with now?'

'Well, the government treated the reef as if it were made out of granite. Something you could blast a hole through, and sit back to enjoy. Only granite is dead stone, while coral is alive. The reef has been gradually rebuilding itself. So whenever the ships come in they sound the channel to see how deep it is.'

'Daddy, I don't like fried plantain. I don't!'

'Oh come on now,' her father snapped. 'You've eaten

75

it for years, and there's no reason why you can't eat it tonight!'

The girl returned sullenly to her plate. Not knowing quite what to say, Rose stared down at the manoeuvering ship. The little boats had just scuttled back to the freighter, and water was boiling at her stern as the old double-stacked ship made all possible steam, and dashed for the harbour.

'She's coming in,' she exclaimed in alarm. The scene looked somewhat like the end of a Hollywood chariot race. The battered old ship kicked up a froth at her bow, scattered the cloud of tiny outrigger canoes that had gone out to meet her, and celebrated her success by a triple blast on her whistle. Rose could see the steam shooting up before she heard the sound. She started to count immediately. 'One thousand one, one thousand two, one thousand three——' and the sound arrived. It was surprisingly deep-throated for such a tired old ship.

'Who taught you that?' He leaned over the table, his lips almost at her ear.

'Why—why I don't know,' she said soberly, trying to avoid contact with him. That little chill ran up her spine again. This amnesiac business isn't as easy as I thought, she told herself. And with just one slip, he—well, I've no idea *what* he would do, and that's the problem. 'Did I do something wrong?'

'No. That's a fine way to measure distance. Sound travels so much slower than light does. And the ship is about three miles away, right?' His cool hawk eyes were on her, ready to pounce at the slightest mistake.

'If you say so,' she sighed.

'I wanna go see the ship,' Josie muttered. 'I really wanna go!'

'Stop nagging,' her father barked. 'We'll go when your mother is ready to go.'

'Oh, please—don't wait for me. It's almost two miles

down there, and two to come back. I'd rather not go all that way. Can't I just wait quietly here, and you and Josie go to enjoy the fun?' It was hard to keep her voice level. Her thoughts were rattling around, ricocheting off each other in their haste to get her attention. This has to be the time, she told herself. While they go down, I can just—just disappear.

'We-ell,' he drawled. 'Yes, it's quite a walk, and you've been busy all day. Okay. You rest and enjoy yourself, and I'll make the sacrifice. Are you sure you can walk that far, Josie?'

'C'mon, Daddy. What an excuse. You know darn well you want to be there, and they'll start unloading tonight, and you'll want to see all the things they bring, and——'

'Okay, okay.' He threw up his hands in defeat. 'Henpecked, that's what I am.'

'Oh, Daddy, that's cornball stuff. I'm ready.'

Rose laughed at them both. It seemed all too easy. What would a mother say now? She reached out and trapped the child's shoulder. 'Whoa up, young lady,' she admonished. 'It will be cold before you come back. Take a shawl to wear. And for goodness sakes, go to the bathroom first.'

They started out fifteen minutes later, laughing as they went. She watched them as they disappeared step-by-step, over her horizon and out of sight. The laughter came floating back on the cool twilight air long after their heads had dropped from sight. Miri came out to clear the table.

'You don't go, *madame?* It is all excitement. You don't go with your man?'

'No, I don't go,' Rose laughed. 'But you do, Miri. You go with *your* man. I'll clean up these things.'

'But, I——'

'Shoo. Go. *Viti viti.*'

'Okay, I go,' the island girl giggled. 'But is the wrong

word. *Viti viti* mean fast. Go fast. Word should be *quickly*. You say *haapeepee*!'

'So I will—*haapeepee*!' Her accent was so terrible that Miri gurgled, but fled down the steps just the same. She turned and waved before she disappeared. Rose returned the wave and laughed at herself. She had been taking daily lessons in the Tahitian dialect of Polynesian. 'And every vowel must be pronounced,' she lectured herself as she followed the movements on the beach across the bay. The little freighter was now making a very cautious approach to the rickety pier. The sun was low on the hills behind her, the mountains of Pele. And it was time for her to go.

Carefully she cleared the table and carried everything back to the kitchen. It took but a moment to scrub and rinse everything under the stream of cool water pouring out of the bamboo pipes. One last look, longingly, around the house. Through his cluttered workroom where papers and books and dust struggled for command, through his bedroom where his clothes were scattered, and then quickly out of the house.

An hour later she had reached a little clearing above the house, and was completely exhausted. She had walked the other mountains earlier. Tuahine, Mona Aui, Mona Atau. They all were girded by neat well-tended paths, so that one had the impression of wandering through a garden. But not here. Pele's Mountain had many trails, but all were overgrown, hardly more than indentations in the tropical growth. The same orange groves, breadfruit trees, vanilla bushes, mangoes all flourished here, but in untouched wild growth. Her every step had been a torture.

Shoes were something she had hardly needed at the Big House, or at the beach. The mountain had frightened her. She borrowed a pair of Miri's rubber Japanese sandals, consisting of a hard sole and a thong which fit between her big toe and its neighbour, to hold them on. In addition to being strange to her, they were a size too big. Her soles were chafed, and the thong was rubbing a blister into being between her toes.

The machete was a total disaster. She had seen it hanging by the kitchen door, and snatched it up at the last minute. The natives used the big knife to cut their way through underbrush. In their hands the blade had swung gracefully and easily. But doing it for herself, she quickly discovered was like trying to decapitate a rattlesnake with a pen knife. Nothing went right. Either she swung the blade too lightly and it bounced off everything, or she swung too hard, and the blade threatened to cut her foot off. In total frustration she started to hurl the heavy knife off the side of the mountain, sloping steeply down behind her. But then she thought again. She had no idea what sorts of wild life might be running free up here. Even the Garden of Eden had snakes, didn't it?

So all in all, when she broke free of the underbrush and came out into the little clearing it was like some gift from the gods. Behind and below here were the trees through which she had been forcing her way. Ahead of her was a sharp deep chasm, looking out on to Pakuo bay. She straggled over to the edge and made herself comfortable on a pile of warm stones. The heat startled her, and then her slow mind reasoned it out. The sun had heated the rocks all day; now it was almost gone. It wasn't the stones that were warm, but the air that was too cold! She stretched herself out flat to absorb some of the warmth while she caught her breath. The cold fingers of the high-altitude breeze toyed with the perspiration on her brow. She shivered.

'So you told Josie to take a shawl,' she told herself sarcastically. 'So where's yours? Idiot! What you need is a mother to look after you!' Or a father, she added silently, or a—husband?

She sat up and wrapped her arms around herself, staring down and out to sea. The mouth of the bay was in shadows. Torches appeared, some stationary, some moving. It made a pretty picture as the quick and silent tropical night fell. She sat there, unmoving, thinking.

Here in this high place she could intuitively feel her father's presence. She *knew* he was alive. Somewhere, somehow, he had come through the storm. She just *knew* it. It was not an unusual feeling. She had for so long been a partner in his life that there was a bond between them. A bond that could not be snapped by distance, condition, or time. And the bond was still tight, still tugging at her, connecting her through the unknown night to her father. She clasped her hands behind her neck and lay back on the flat of the stones, smiling.

Time passed. Unmeasurable time. The dog-star was plodding downhill into the west. The moon threatened to rise in the distant east, over towards Tahiti, and down below she could hear conch-shell trumpets sounding. She sat up to look. At the pier flares guided a line of workers going back and forth like worker ants. But there were other flares out in the night. Up along the heights of Mona Atau, across the ridge between the Two Sisters. Sets of widely spaced lights, they flickered and wove patterns, as if the whole village was moving in the night.

A trembling fear locked on to her spirits. They were searching for her! The police authority had called out the whole village to find her! Desperation drove. She stumbled to her feet, flexed her stiff muscles, and forced them to take her farther up the mountain, deep into the dark jungle again, and then finally, out on to the lava lip where nothing grew.

She was looking down again, directly into the crater of the volcano where, in some distant past, Pele's mountain had blown her top off and sent molten lava streaming down toward the bay below. The cavity was in darkness. The moon was not yet high enough to dig a path into the crater area. Give it a few minutes more, she told herself. Just a few minutes, and there'll be light. She was shaking again, but not from the cold. She slumped down on to the crumbling lava bed, wrapping her arms around herself to stay the shaking that was tearing her to pieces. She turned around to look back in the direction from which she had come.

Below her, very far away now, the flares were light-points at the dock area. A fading fire twinkled here and there in the village. The mountains were dark. She could not see the Big House, hidden from her under the curve of the mountains. One lonely tear trickled down her cheek.

By now the moon had topped the jagged edge of the crater, lighting paths, casting shadows. Rose took a deep breath. Her leg muscles almost refused her command to move. A well-marked trail wound its way down into the open maw. She plunged ahead, staggering carelessly. The rubber sandals slipped on the crumpling lava rock. Slip and you're dead, you poor fool! In one careless minute you can be off the edge! Down into that— she stopped and steadied herself against a rock outcropping. The silver fingers of the moon had touched the surface of the crater, where glittering silver-painted water gleamed at her, roiled slightly by a tiny breeze. There was a lake in the crater, and not many yards below her!

She struggled with her breathing, trying to steady her nerves. A few more yards. Only a few. She stepped carefully, testing the path with her foot before entrusting her weight to it. Down, and farther down. And the trail ended. She was on a flat plateau that served as the shore of this miracle lake, and near at hand, to her right, the mouth of a huge cave opened. She groped for it, found a great flat rock at its mouth, and dropped down on it, moaning her relief. Her feet contacted something in the shadows, and displaced it. It fell to the sand at the foot of the rock with a dull thud.

The slight breeze that blew over her was warmer, much warmer than she had felt on the outer lip of the mountain. And she was tired, desperately tired. She coiled herself up on the rock, opened her ears to the gentle lapping of wavelets in the lake, and closed her eyes.

Visions flashed across her inner eyelids. Black and white images. Her father, waving, a cheerful grin on his too-handsome face, but safe. Little Josie, staring directly at her, her mouth twisted in agony, screaming 'Please don't leave me, Mommy!' And then Giles. His deep-furrowed face marked with concerns, problems—searching—for what? Her mind had no answer but she clung to this last image as if it were a life line. What worried Giles? What was it about the coming of the police that *he* was concerned about? Why did he insist that she was his wife, that Josie was her natural daughter? Why was it, when he was so remote, so cool, she was afraid of him? The puzzle was too deep for her tired mind. She gave up the struggle.

She slept fitfully until it grew suddenly warmer, and then she slept soundly. When she awoke she was in deep shadow. The sun was up, but not high enough to light the crater. There was a robe thrown over her. An old ceremonial robe, plaited with feathers. And a little distance away, an old man, squatting by a tiny fire. The *tahu'a*. He was roasting something on a stick. She sat up. The movement caught his eye. He smiled, got up, and came over to her with the stick.

'*Tamahine?*' He came around the flat stone platform on which she rested, but did not touch it. 'You eat?' He offered her the roast. She held up both hands in a repulsing gesture. Her few weeks on Tahiti had taught her that no mere *vahine* ate in front of a *tahu'a*—but then, he knew that, didn't he? Then why did he offer?

He smiled, showing a mouthful of perfect teeth. 'No *tapuus* here,' he chuckled. 'This is Pele's place. Here only is a man and a woman, and this foolish plover. Eat.' He stripped a section of meat from the roast and nibbled on it, all the while extending the stick to her. Trembling, she followed suit. The meat, rich in juices, trickled down her throat and revived her. The old man squatted down in front of the rock and dissected the remainder of the bird.

'The man,' he offered, after considerable gnawing. 'He fears for you. All over the island they search, but nobody would come up here. You heard Pele call, no?' He gestured towards the rock. There was enough light for Rose to see where she was. It was not really a rock, but rather a carefully assembled stone platform, with stones intricately cut to notch into each other. She scrambled off on to the sand, dragging the feather cape behind her.

'Oh Lord,' she sighed. 'It's a *maere*? A Sacred Platform?'

The old man laughed and nodded. 'Built for Pele. This is her place.' He waved a hand around the circle of the crater. 'She called and you came, no?'

'I—I don't know,' Rose stammered. 'Nobody called. Nobody believes in that stuff any more. I just didn't—I couldn't—my husband, he——'

'The man? He is not your husband. Not yet.' The old man spoke softly, every word flowing like a liquid. 'And of course. Nobody believes. That is all—what you Americans call—mumbo jumbo! Eat.'

'You know that he——'

'I know,' the old man laughed. 'The real business of a *tahu'a* is to know things. Everything. The man wrestles with his own terrible problem, and you wrestle with your own terrible problem—but you do *not* know—you are sent here because of Pele's terrible problem. And when you and he solve Pele's problem, you also solve your own!'

'Nonsense! That's all—what you said. Mumbo jumbo.' He doesn't know anything, she told herself fiercely. Not anything. He's only an old man. A doddering old man! Him and his crazy goddesses! He was smiling sympathetically at her, almost as if he could read her mind.

'Just an old man,' he chuckled. 'Just dreams, no?'

'I—I——' She struggled for some soft explanation that would not hurt, and found none. It didn't seem to bother the old man. He settled himself into a more comfortable position, and offered her the rest of the roast. Without thinking about it, she accepted. He wiped his fingers clean in the sand.

'I am old,' he mused. 'When I was young there were great times, *Tamahine*. There was the great war, no? Americans came to Bora Bora. Thousands of them. They brought books, radios, dreams, airplanes, electricity, babies. I saw it all. And then they went home, and the islands were empty of them. They took their generators, their airplanes, their God, but not their children. We wanted the children.

'Then I went to Papeete, Honolulu, Samoa. Everywhere the *popa'a* touched, the Polynesian ways died. So at last I came here to Tuahine. Pele no longer thunders, and Tangora no longer raises the waves, they say. But since we only have our dreams, why should I not cling to them, no?'

'I—you really believe in the old religion?' she stammered.

'Believe? Perhaps. Why not? Pele lives. Tangora lives. She no longer screams for the blood of sacrifice; he no longer rules the war canoes. We have all come to our elder days, Pele and I. But many of the old habits are left. Did you know that if a *vahine* sleeps on Pele's *maere* that all her dreams will be true?' He looked up at her with a very sharp eye. She ducked her head to hide the blushes. In the moments before she had awakened she had dreamed again. Strange dreams, that sent her writhing in her sleep, moaning. Dreams about Giles Gendron. Dreams about—Lord, *that* could never come true! She shook herself to regain control, and the old man laughed. She dug her teeth into the remainder of the roast and tore it from the stick.

'The man—he wants you,' the *tahu'a* said. He got to his feet and brushed himself down.

'For some scheme,' she snapped back at him through a mouth half-filled with meat. 'He doesn't *want* me. He *needs* me. There's a difference. And I don't know why he needs me.' The last sentence came out wistfully.

'Old men learn some things ' he said solemnly. 'He wants you. Walk carefully *Tamahine*. You have an errand to do. I go down to tell them you are safe. You will come?'

'When the boat leaves,' she answered. 'I—when the boat leaves.'

'When the boat leaves.' He nodded as if the explanation were very clear to him. And then he turned away and plodded up the path, into the bright sunlight, and out of sight. She sat back, remembering the glint of of sunlight on his pure white hair.

'Fortune-telling,' she told herself forcefully. 'Nothing but fortune-telling. Hah!' But she could not repress the uneasy feeling that came to her. All my dreams will come true? Dad is alive and well? Josie will cry over me? Giles will drive me mad in his bed? Stuff!

But it was worth a thought at that, she told herself, as she walked around to the front of Pele's *maere*. It was worth a thought. I'm twenty years old, going on one hundred. I've been my father's nursemaid since mother died. Seven years, with hardly a chance to meet a—some young people. I've been so busy being my father's shadow that I haven't had a chance to be me. Why, I don't even know who *me* is!

It was at that point that her swinging foot touched the little stone figure lying in the sand. And somehow or another she remembered. The little statue had been standing at the front lip of the *maere* when she sprawled down on it during the night, and her foot had knocked it off into the sand. She bent over and picked up the little figure. Hardly more than a foot long, the soft stone had been given the likeness of a crouching woman, her hands clasped around her knees, her huge breasts protruding. Where the face should be was a worn blank. It looked to be a thousand years old. A *tiki*! She smiled at the idea, just as the sun's rays penetrated the crater wall and sparkled over her and her new find.

A real *tiki*! She had heard enough in her few weeks in Papeete to recognise it as one of the symbols of the Old Religion. Dedicated to some minor goddess, she told herself. Ancient. Valueless. The islands were full of little *tiki*s. But this one's mine! She cuddled it in her arms and started back out of the crater.

It was easier going than it had been coming. The paths seemed to be better marked going downhill. Within the hour she was back at the little outcropping where she had stopped to rest the night before. She crept quietly back to the edge of the cliff and looked down. The village was sleepily quiet. The dock was empty. Out some distance beyond the reef she could see a pillar of smoke that marked the position of the old freighter.

'And that settles that,' she told her little world, with a vast sigh of relief. 'The boat's gone, and the policeman with it, so that does it!' She held up her little statue to let it see the sight. Now I *am* being a fool, she chided herself as she started down towards the Big House. Playing with dolls, no less! Nevertheless she cradled the little stone figure in the shelter of her arm, and was singing as she stumbled out of the last clump of trees above the house.

'My God, woman, where the hell have you been!' Giles grabbed her by both arms and swung her around, back into the trees. He almost jarred her little *tiki* out of her arms.

'Don't do that,' she snapped. 'You're hurting me!'

'Hurting you? You don't know what hurting means. Not yet, you don't,' he snarled. 'It took me half the night to get Inspector Tihoni to bed. And if it hadn't been for that damn *tahu'a* I don't know what kind of a story I would have concocted.'

'You're good at stories,' she hissed at him. 'Let go of me!'

His hands dropped to his sides. 'Okay, okay.' His face was pale, his eyes haunted. 'I've got a lot riding on this visit. The *tahu'a* said you were up in the mountain, tracing some ancient stone work. It sounded good. The Inspector bought it. Stick to it.'

'I'm sure you could have thought of something better!' She put all of her disdain into the statement. 'I was communing with Pele, or something like that?'

'Damn,' he muttered.

'What?'

'That's what the *tahu'a* said. His exact words. You were communing with Pele. Did you really meet that old fake up on the mountain?'

'If you mean the *tahu'a*, yes. He may be old, but he's not a fake. And we talked. Now that I think of it, his story made a hell of a lot more sense than the line you've been feeding me!'

He grabbed at her elbow this time. 'Just what in hell do you mean by that smart remark,' he snapped. Her jaw fell open. She had never in the world intended to make such a statement. The policeman might have gone with the freighter, but all ships had radios!

'I—I didn't mean anything, really,' she sighed. 'I'm tired. It was cold up on that mountain. I'm hungry.'

'Well, I should hope so,' he growled. 'Into the house.

And remember who the devil you are, Mrs Gendron!'
He took her arm again, a shade more gently than
before, and hurried her the last few steps to the house.
She stumbled a couple of times, and the thong of her
sandals rubbed against yesterday's bruises and blisters.
He left her on the veranda.

'Get yourself a shower and get cleaned up,' he said
coldly. 'I'll be in the dining room.'

I'll be in the dining room! She mimicked under her
breath. The colossal nerve of the man. Snap to, female.
Here are your marching orders! Oh Lord, I wish I were
six-feet-five and could beat him up the way he deserves!
But it was only wishing. She hurried down the corridor
and into her room. There were strange things strewn
around the room. Packages, and men's clothing. She
shook her head to clear it. Sleeping on the stone *maere*
had not been all that restful. My brain must be addled,
she sighed to herself. Maybe I *am* Mrs Gendron. Maybe
my amnesia is real? Nonsense!

She fumbled around in the confusion and managed
to find herself something to wear. A *pareau*, a pair of
soft slippers. She set the stone *tiki* down on the bedside
table, picked up her chosen clothing, and hurried off to
the bathroom. Hurry, one side of her brain told her. He
said hurry! Why, the other side of her brain queried.
Just because that—that arrogant man said so? Hah! It
required a great deal of determination, but she slowed
down. Why is it so hard, she asked herself. Why?
Because I'm afraid of that man? Lord, what's come
over me lately. Rose Lambert was never ever afraid of
anything or anybody—well, almost never. Her lip
twitched in laughter. Almost never. She ducked into the
bathroom, shed her dirty clothes, and went into the
shower stall.

The warmth of the water was comforting. It was not
sun-hot as it would be later in the day, but it was warm
enough. She lathered extravagantly in the coconut-oil

soap, rubbing vigorously, singing. A voice sounded from just outside the shower curtain.

'Mamma?' There were volatile tears in the voice. Rose reached over and flipped the curtain back. There were tears in the eyes, too. Big round ripe tears, dropping one after the other from those lovely little eyes. Josie.

'What is it, love?' It was impossible to hide the affection in her husky contralto voice, and she really didn't want to. Her hands kept up their rhythmic massage, moving large globules of soapsuds around on her body, but her mind was engrossed in the scene before her. The dreams. My Papa is alive, Josie is crying over me, and *he* wants me! 'Josie?'

'I——' The little girl leaned against the steel frame of the shower. 'I couldn't find you. You didn't sleep in bed, and I thought you went away on the boat! I couldn't find you, and Daddy was so mad he just yelled at me, and I thought I—Mamma?'

There was only one way to answer that appeal. Rose held out both soap-splattered arms, and the child ran into them, soap and all. The little head buried itself just under her breasts, and the salt tears ran down across her abdomen. They clung to each other like a couple of castaways on a raft. Until the little girl sputtered and began to laugh.

'I think I got soap in my mouth,' she spouted. 'I'm all over soap!' But the tears had stopped, and there was a glitter of happiness in those wide eyes.

'Might as well not waste it,' Rose laughed. 'Here, slip out of that dress and we'll both rinse off together.' Small fingers hastened, and in a moment they were both nude. Rose flicked the shower curtain shut. 'Ready?' she asked.

'Ready,' Josie giggled. 'Only I think I'll hug you some more?'

'Of course, love.' With one of her hands entangled in

the girl's hair, Rose used the other to pull on the chain controlling the shower. Rinse water poured over them. They did a crazy little dance around the shower stall, and sang a silly song Rose remembered from her own childhood. And when the three-minute spray halted they were both glowing.

'We have to get some more bigger towels,' she told her daughter as they struggled with the little hand-towels that hung on the rack. My daughter! That's really how I think of her, isn't it. My daughter. Too bad that she comes as a package with that—that man. We could be very happy together, Josie·and her mother!

'Daddy said he was ordering——' The little girl stopped her wagging tongue by plastering both hands across her mouth.

'Daddy said?'

'Daddy said keep my mouth shut,' the little girl answered, chagrined. 'And I almost gave the whole thing away, didn't I? I'm not very good at this secret business.'

'Me neither,' Rose giggled. 'Turn around here now while I dry your hair. You haven't been shampooing enough lately. You've still got sand in the base of your hair. Tch.'

'Tch? What does that mean?'

'It means, little love, that as I look you over more carefully, I can see that your mother doesn't take care of you well enough. And it also means that you're a long way from being six years old. Just look at you!'

'Is it bad, the way I look? I gotta be six. At least for three more days I gotta be six!'

Rose shook her head, laughing. 'No, love. It all looks very nice. Very nice indeed. But if you have to play six years old for another three days we'd better keep you covered up. Me too, for that matter. Suppose you run and get each of us one of those *muumuu*'s that I made. The red and green and gold ones. And I think you'd better hurry. I suspect your father is angry with me, and he's waiting!'

'Mommy?' When I get bigger will I look like you?'

'Well, perhaps not entirely, love. God puts growing orders—a genetic code we call it—in each of us when we're born. I guess you'll still look somewhat like me. We have the same colour hair, the same eyes, you know.'

'I didn't mean like that. I mean, like, you're all curvy and soft, and like that. Will I?'

'Ah. I can't tell that, love. *My* mother was all slender and *chic*, and look how I turned out. I'm too—well, there's too much of me.'

'Daddy don't think so.'

'Daddy doesn't?'

'Nope. Yesterday I was teasing him, and I said, boy, have we got us a lot of Mommy there! And he said yes—isn't it wonderful That's what he said.'

'Hey, that's enough of *that* talk. Scoot.' Rose turned the girl around and gave her bottom a tap in the right direction. 'Hurry up.' The girl scooted, missing the flashing blush that spread from Rose's oval face all over her delightfully curved body.

Dressed demurely in all-covering loose *muumuus*, the two delayed just a moment in Rose's bedroom while she displayed her new find. 'That's cute,' Josie said. 'You can't hardly see nothin', and yet it looks like—well, I don't know what it looks like. What is it?'

'It's a *tiki*,' she explained. 'In the old days Polynesians used them to mark their temples, to stand in for their gods, and things like that.'

'That's not a god,' Josie commented solemnly. 'No way!'

'Perhaps not,' Rose offered. 'She's definitely a female, isn't she. You like it?' The child nodded. 'I'm going to keep it here in my room. I'm not sure your father will approve of the idea, but I'm going to anyway.'

'We better go have breakfast,' the girl reminded her. 'Why don't you bring it with you and show them.'

'Them?' Rose was busy wrapping the little statue up in a *pareau*, covering it from head to foot.

'Yeah. We got company for breakfast. You missed everything. Where was you?'

'I—I went up the mountain,' Rose offered softly. 'Come on, let's go see just how angry your father is!' She scooped up the offered hand in one of hers, and used the other to pick up the packaged statue. They both skipped as they went down the hall. At least they did until Rose's feet reminded her of their poor condition. There was nobody in the dining room.

'*Iorana*,' Miri sang out from the kitchen. 'They decide to eat on the veranda. You like eggs for breakfast?'

'Eggs? Where in the world did we get eggs?'

'The boat comes, of course. Powdered eggs, you understand, but they make nice scrambled?'

'You bet,' Rose called back. 'Anything!'

The two of them wheeled around, went out the front door to the shady side of the porch, and came to a dead halt. Giles was standing there beside the laden table making small talk with a massive Polynesian man. He was dressed in the lightweight uniform of the Island police.

'I——' Rose struggled to run, but the little girl's hand anchored her. Giles was talking with his hands, the typical method of island cross-language conversations. A look in the policeman's eyes caught his attention, and he turned.

'Ah! Rose!' He came over to her, taking her hand from Josie's, and towing her over to the table. 'Rose,' he offered the introduction, 'this is Inspector Tihoni from Tahiti. My wife Rose, and this is my daughter Josie.'

The big man rose and sported a smile all over his bronze face. '*Madame*.' It was a cultural shock she was not prepared for, hearing the almost-perfect French coming from this almost-perfect Polynesian giant. And then English, equally as good. 'We heard that *Madame* is interested in the old ways, no?'

Rose shrugged her shoulders helplessly. Now it comes, she told herself bitterly. 'Are you Rose Lambert,' he would say next. 'You're under arrest for having a father who steals money, Rose Lambert!'

'I—I,' she stammered, and got no further.

'Sit down, Mommy.' Josie was holding a chair for her. She offered a weak smile of thanks and sank down into it. Come on, her brain nagged at her. Go on the offensive. If he hasn't the time to say 'Are you Rose Lambert,' he'll never be able to arrest me!

'My mommy's been sick.' Josie stepped close to her side and gave the policeman a fierce protective look. 'You gotta be careful when you talk with her. You make her cry and I'll——' Two little fists were raised threateningly. Rose gulped for breath, and quelled the mutiny by sweeping Josie up into her lap.

'Yes,' she said, her words pouring out as if a dam had burst. 'We—my daughter and I—we're interested in the old ways. This is my daughter.' She pulled Josie closer, bending the little face down beside her own. Establish an identity, her mind screamed at her. Quickly!

'And that, of course, is what I came to find out,' the police officer offered in a friendly manner. Startled, Rose leaned back away from him, her face turning pale. *That's* what he came all this way to find out? Why?

'In Papeete there is some doubt, you will understand, about whose daughter she is. The American Consul is most insistent that we find out. And now of course, my eyes tell me. She is certainly your daughter, no? The hair, the eyes, the smile. Of course!' He beamed at them all.

Gendron beamed back at him, then came over and

rested an arm on Rose's shoulder. 'Perfect,' he said. 'Perfect.'

Not willing still to let the officer get those fatal words in, Rose babbled on. 'We—I—last night, I found something on the mountain,' she rattled, putting the wrapped package on the table in front of her. 'And I thought—I knew I—well, I brought it down because it shouldn't be lying up there on the side of the mountain, and——' While her tongue wagged on her brain began to function. He came about Josie? But it's all right because Josie is my daughter? What's going on here? What in the world is . . .

Miri interrupted. She carried out a loaded tray that smelled like heaven. Ham and eggs, Rose's nose told her. How long has it been since I had ham and eggs. And—good Lord—bread!

'Flour. Also from the boat,' the Polynesian girl whispered in her ear. 'While it lasts, we have bread!'

'Iorana!' Another voice with the Polynesian greeting. Rose looked down, off the porch. The *tahu'a* stood there, proud in the crown of his white hair, his *pareau* slung gracefully at his hips. 'So you came, *Tamahine*. Good. Everything will be!'

That was all he said. Everything will be! Rose lifted her dazed eyes to Giles. This whole conversation had long since run far over her head. Her *husband* was looking back at her. Not like a hawk about to strike. More like a—a lover? A warm cheerfulness had erased the worry furrows on his face, and had left him almost—almost handsome. The corner of his mouth was twitching, as if he were fighting off laughter. Quickly she swivelled to the policeman. His solemn eyes were following her fingers, which were slow unwrapping the *tiki*.

He's such a big man, she thought, some of her fear returning. He'll just grab me by the scruff of the neck and drag me down to the—'Oh Lord, the ship has sailed.'

'Until the day after tomorrow,' the Inspector offered. 'There is one more stop in the chain of islands, you know. *Motu One*. But I have no reason to go to that island, so I wait here. It stops here on the way back.'

And then he'll do it, her mind rattled on. Then he'll do it! Do they put manacles on woman prisoners? Why am I so frightened of him? First it was Giles I was afraid of, and now it's the policeman. He's so big. He's AUTHORITY! He'll just—and she stared at the policeman, in shock. Her fingers had finally unveiled the little statue.

Inspector Tihoni's eyes shifted, flared, and a look of surprise flashed across his face. He pushed back his chair and backed away from the table to the very edge of the veranda. Giles looked at him with astonishment. The old *tahu'a* cackled. The big burly policeman pointed a heavy finger at the little statue.

'*Sacré Bleu!* Pele!' he half-shouted. He took one more step backward, and fell off the end of the veranda.

CHAPTER SIX

THE old *tahu'a* was laughing as he helped the Inspector back on to his feet. 'On no,' he said. 'Nobody in the islands believe in the old gods. Nobody. That is correct, Inspector?'

'Of course. No one believes in such superstitions. We are a modern people.' The policeman was having trouble with the collar of his uniform. It might have been too tight. Well, at least *something's* making him turn all mottled red, Rose told herself.

'Then this—this statue of Pele is just an old superstition?'

'Just so,' the inspector told her. 'It—surprised me, nothing more.' Just the same, when he resumed his seat at the table he made sure he was as far from the ugly little *tiki* as he could get.

'There is a mistake,' the *tahu'a* said. He was staring straight at Rose, as if trying to impress something of great importance on her mind. 'This is not a statue, *Tamahine*. This is Pele herself. You brought Pele down from the mountain.' He smiled as if it were a good joke—that only the two of them could share. Inspector Tihoni seemed to turn pale, and Moera, who had come out on to the veranda with another platter just in time to hear his words, dropped the entire load, screamed, and ran back to the kitchen. No amount of coaxing would bring her back.

'I think I'd better put her away,' Rose sighed, and instantly lectured herself. Don't you have enough troubles of your own, she snarled. Why do you let this—this witch doctor convince you that—put *her* away. Now he's got *you* believing it! She appealed to

96

Giles silently. He nodded his approval, and gave her a quirky little grin. She tried out a tentative return smile, and felt rather pleased because it seemed to work. She scooped up the *pareau* in which Pele had originally been wrapped, and made up another package.

'Josie,' she said softly, 'take this into Mamma's room and set it on the table please. And come right back to this wonderful breakfast!'

The *tahu'a* watched the little girl run into the house with her burden. He laughed, a very satisfied laugh. The Inspector watched too, and gave a huge sigh of relief when she disappeared down the hall.

'And now breakfast,' Rose said firmly. 'What can I serve you?' She offered first to the old Polynesian. It seemed only proper. He represented the oldest authority. He made a small selection among the fruits, accepted the coffee, and had two of the deliciously light croissants that the girls had produced. The other men made their selections, and by the time Josie came back all were eating.

The little girl slipped into the chair beside Rose, offered a big smile, and began with her ham and eggs. Rose wrinkled her nose at her, tapped gently at the elbows on the table, and dug in for herself. After a satisfactory time the police officer cleared his throat, brought out a notebook, and looked around expectantly.

'It will require a report,' he stated, and then sighed. 'Everything requires a report. Now then—the little girl is named?'

'Excuse me.' It's gone far enough, Rose told herself. Another minute of this and I'll go right through the roof. I *have* to know what the devil is going on!

The Inspector paused, notebook open, pen ready, and waited for her to continue.

'I——' she stuttered. A deep breath steadied her nerves. 'Why? Why must there be a report. What do you want to—what's going on here! What! For God's sake, somebody tell me before I lose my mind!'

'Ah!' The policeman capped his pen and seemed to find something terribly important to examine on the table top. After a moment he lifted his head again. '*Madame* has been sick, no?'

'My wife sustained a head injury,' Giles interrupted nervously. 'Sometimes she—forgets. And we didn't want to worry her, so I didn't tell her about—anything.'

'But I have to know,' Rose demanded fiercely. 'I can't—you have to tell me!'

'Yes.' The Inspector had decided on his next course of action. 'I am come, *Madame* Gendron, because we receive from the United States, through Paris, you understand, a most formal complaint. There is a charge of to kidnap. A child has been stolen in New York, from the home of her mother. A terrible thing, no?' He took another sip at his coffee cup, considering his next few words. 'There is a—a break in the home——'

'A broken home,' Giles interjected. His face had turned to stone, his voice the same.

'*Merci.* The broken home, of course. There is the divorce, no? And the court has said to the mother, take the child. But—well—this terrible charge from the Americans say that the father have come to this house in New York, have committed breakage to enter, assault, battery, and have kidnap this child. So will the Police in Tahiti please to investigate this *Monsieur* Giles Gendron to see if he has taken this child. Now——' He uncapped his pen again, took one more tug at the coffee cup. 'This little girl, her name is?'

'Josie,' Rose offered, very tentatively. She had *heard* the explanation, but had not reasoned it out.

'Josie Rose Gendron,' the child recited. Rose gulped quickly and flashed a look at Giles. He returned one of injured innocence. The Inspector wrote busily in his book.

'And her age is?'

'Six!' All three of them spoke in unison. 'I'm six years old,' the child repeated.

'And the mother's name?'

'Rose,' she told him, fighting against the weight of a pair of suddenly-heavy eyelids. 'Rose Harriet—Gendron.'

The Inspector scribbled diligently. 'And the child was born where?'

'San Francisco,' Rose sighed, having no real idea what the truth might be.

'Portland, Oregon,' Josie hurried to get in.

'Right here,' Giles growled, doing his best to out-shout everybody. 'Right her on Te Tuahine.'

'There is some—disagreement?'

'Not at all,' Giles insisted. 'I told you about my wife's—small illness. The child was born here. Monsieur Apuka can show you the records.'

'Yes, of course. Right here.' For some reason Rose felt she had to support the claim, but her mind was in a complete whirl. Not only was she receiving more—facts—than she cared to know, but she was also beginning to tire.

'Ah.' More scribbling in the Inspector's book, and then he closed it and carefully put his pen away in his pocket. 'And so obviously then, it is not possible that this child could be ten years old, by the name of Caroline, eh?'

Josie started to say something, and her father pressed his leg against hers under the table. All three of the *Gendrons* presented a united front, smiling at the policeman. 'No, of course not,' Giles said very conclusively.

'And this other child,' the Inspector mused. 'You are not concerned that this other child of yours is missing?'

'Of course I am!'

Rose settled back in her chair, and waited to see how

the scheming conniver would work his way out of *this* little corner. 'But I don't know what I can do about it,' Giles continued. 'I don't have any money. My former wife gets it all in alimony payments. Are you *sure* this isn't something that she arranged?'

The policeman laughed. '*Cherchez la femme*—in fact, two of them?' He raised an eyebrow, and chuckled. 'No, monsieur, we do not know such a thing, nor can we find out. It is a matter for the Americans. We act here only out of—friendship—with them. They say, look in Tahiti for a ten year old girl stolen from her mother. And instead we find a happy family, a father, a mother, and a six year old girl. The government of Tahiti will do nothing to disturb a happy family, you understand!' He thumped the table to make his point.

And by this time some of the data was beginning to make sense in Rose's tired mind. Why—why that dirty—that rat! She turned to stare at Giles. Waves of anger pulsed at her throat, flushing her face. He could see it all. That's what he's using me for, she screamed to herself. I'm just trying to avoid a little—unpleasant-ness—about fifty thousand embezzled francs. *He's* wanted for kidnapping! And making me into a surrogate mother just to support his dirty underhanded conniving . . . Ahh!

The policeman came for *him*, not for me. And Giles took one look at the poor little amnesiac, and set me up in the middle of a kidnapping charge! Lord, what a naïve little lamb I've been. Damn the man! Her two small hands balled into fists. She placed them carefully on the edge of the table behind her plate, wishing she had the nerve to thump and rant and rattle. Josie snuggled a little closer, and used her own hands to cover her 'mother's'. The warmth of the little body against her side partially restored her control. That, and the little wandering truth that managed to surface on top of all her anger. You *could* rant and rave and rattle, little

Miss Lambert, if only you hadn't been so damn busy trying to con *him* at the same time!

'So,' the policeman continued. 'That settles that little problem. Now, I have a hundred boring things to do. I must check the register of births and deaths and marriages, and make a health inspection of the copra gathering, and all the other things a government wishes to know, *ehe*? And perhaps, since I am empowered, we might celebrate a few civil marriages. Who knows?' He stood up, all the magnificence of his Polynesian forebears outlined in a French police uniform. 'Isn't it strange,' he mused, looking over at Rose. 'Twice in two weeks I deal with a case where a woman is named Rose Harriet.'

'Twice?' she asked weakly. Don't ask, her conscience barked at her. Stupid woman, don't ask! You not only don't want to know, but you don't even want him to think about it!

'That's quite a coincidence,' Giles said, rising with his guest. 'Another Rose Harriet?'

'Just so,' the policeman nodded. 'Hard to believe, no? Rose Harriet Lambert. A very involved case. Arson, embezzlement, storms at sea, an important witness, shipwrecks, and Rose Lambert is missing. Oh well, it is hoped that she will turn up, but—the ocean is very big, and the islands very small.' He waved a hand to them and, in company with the *tahu'a*, started down towards the beach and the village.

Everything is coming unstuck, Rose sighed to herself. Just for a moment there, I thought I was home free. Just for a moment. But no, I had to be stupid enough to give him my right name. Where else in all the Pacific would there be a young blonde named Rose Harriet. Stupid, stupid, stupid! But what did he say? *Arson* and embezzlement? What in the world does that have to do with anything. And how come he said Rose Lambert was missing? Because they've found Papa?

It was all too much. One weary hand pushed her plate aside, the other made a little nest on the table, and her head came down into it. Before the Inspector had disappeared from sight she was fast asleep, drawn deep into the cavern where fears could not follow her.

'She's gone to sleep,' Josie whispered when they turned back from watching their departing guests. 'Just like that, she's fallen asleep!' To Josie, falling asleep was a complicated endeavour, requiring squirming, story-reading, a doll to squeeze, and a bed on which to sprawl. It wasn't something one did while sitting at the breakfast table!

'Yes,' her father said softly. 'The poor girl is exhausted! All night up on the mountain, and then all this.' He put an arm around his daughter and squeezed her. 'But she did royally well for us, didn't she? I don't think we have any more reason to worry about your mother chasing us. At least not for a year or two.'

'Rose *is* my mother,' the little girl snapped at him. 'Her. That one right there. I don't have another mother. And I don't want another mother!'

'Hey, baby.' He cuddled her closer, but over her shining head he was looking at the sleeping woman. Something was touching his heart. There's a whole lot of woman there, he told himself. A lot of loving and care, and—my God, what a figure! Is it only because I've not seen a white woman in two years?

'We hafta keep Rose!' His daughter had backed away from him, and her beautiful green eyes were demanding a pledge. One that he was not sure he could make or keep. 'We *hafta*!' For just a second he felt the same way. Yes, we *do* have to keep her! But he set the thought aside.

'She's not a toy or a pet,' he said solemnly. 'She's very—nice. But probably she has people of her own, and a place to go to. Hey, precious, for all we know she may be married and have children of her own.'

'But if she didn't, Daddy? Could we keep her?'

He withdrew into a typical parental defence. 'Ask me again later,' he said. 'Right now we've got to get your mother to bed. You run ahead and open things up while I carry her inside.'

She stirred when he slipped his arms under her knees and lifted her off the chair. Her head lolled back against his shoulder, and she snuggled down under his chin. She was no light weight, but he had expected that. A whole lot of woman, a pocket Venus! That ancient male stirring ran up through his blood. Damning himself, he let his upper arm shift slightly, until his massive hand cupped the softness of her breast. She moved slightly, closer to him, and smiled in her sleep. It was too much to ask, that his hand move away, he told himself. Too damn much to ask. As he carried her down the hall, that hand flexed against the firm softness of her, and the stirrings ran riot in him, even as he lectured himself about taking advantage of her.

His daughter was standing beside the stripped bed, holding one finger over her lips in a shushing motion. He got a grip on himself and lowered the woman to the bed. One gentle hand slipped off her sandals, the other moved to the hem of her *muumuu* before common sense intervened.

'Go ask Miri to come and undress your mother,' he ordered gruffly. The girl nodded and vanished. Isn't that strange, he asked himself. She's as stubborn a spoiled little minx as you might ask for, but tell her to do something for her *mother* and she's away like a shot!

He stared down at the face of the woman on the bed. Sleep had stolen away all her defences. She lay there in a seductive sprawl, a lovely smile on her face, her hair scattered in disarray across the pillow. Unable to control himself, he let his hand wander through the golden silk, spreading it out carefully, combing it with stiff fingers. She stirred again and the smile disappeared. He snatched his hand back, and then, driven, bent over and kissed her full on the lips. Miri came into the room as he did so.

'*Aue*,' the island girl whispered. 'I thought there is a mistake. Why you want *me* to undress your wife. You will do that for yourself? *Nehenehe*, that one.'

'Yes, she *is* beautiful,' he sighed, moving away. 'But you'd better undress her, Miri. I have to get back to work!'

'Strange, you *popa'ae*,' the girl chuckled. 'A beautiful *vahine* of your own, and you have to go back to work?'

He worked hard all afternoon, until the sun slanted in the windows, and he knew it was close to five o'clock. He looked around at the scattering of pages on the desk, the table, and the floor. It had been a fruitful afternoon. All his juices were flowing. As they have to be, he reminded himself. Helen cleaned us out, and we've spent the advance from this book already. It *has* to be a best seller. We need the money! And this one ought to do it. High adventure, high sex, an exotic background—Lord, I can almost taste the movie rights! He was smiling as he turned off his little machine and covered it.

He left the papers still strewn around the room. That was his little fetish. He would straighten them all out tomorrow, before he started off at the keyboard again. That overnight 'seasoning' was what brought him all his luck. And that's what a successful writer needs. Perception, language, and luck! He was smiling as he stepped out into the hall.

A breeze from the north was blowing into her room, sending the drapes at the doorway billowing out into the corridor. He stopped and looked in. She was sprawled out on her back, outlined under the thin sheet that almost covered her. Her hair surrounded her head like a halo. The sheet followed her form lovingly, sagging between her wide-spread legs and outlining her hips and thighs in all their fullness. She half-turned in her sleep, and the cover fell away from one full ivory breast. The bronze tip captured his whole attention. Immediately he could feel that surge of impatient maleness coursing through his blood. He could not free his eyes from that roseate nub, standing there on the peak of its alabaster mountain, challenging him. His feet carried him across the room. He moved like a sleepwalker, unable to control his own passions. Across the room, to the side of the bed.

He dropped to his knees, inches away from temptation. She moaned slightly in her sleep, and moved. That one perfect breast quivered slightly, and was still. His mind commanded him to go—to get up and run before he spoiled everything. You need this woman's co-operation, he hammered at himself. You need her to complete the deception. And now you know something more about her too. There couldn't possibly be two women in the islands named Rose Harriet. So that makes you Rose Harriet Lambert, little lovely, with all the police on the lookout for you! Get up and leave, his mind yelled at him.

Little woman, hah! His eyes were feeling a peculiar strain. His hands actually moved to help him push himself up and away. But they moved only an inch or two, coming to rest on the edge of the mattress. And instead it was his head that moved. It bent forward slowly, until his lips surrounded the beautiful bud that faced him. Surrounded and gently tasted with his rough tongue until the softness hardened and thrust at him. He looked up at her. Her eyes had snapped open, filled with—what?

She was caught up in those milliseconds between sleep and awakening, when the rapid eye movement indicated a dream in progress. It was a wild screaming dream, filled with enormities—and Giles. The two of them, intertwined in hot passion, clinging to each other, naked, striving each to arouse the other. Until suddenly he touched her breast with his lips, and the dream shattered. It left her bereft, unsatiated, awake. And staring at him.

'What—what are you doing!' Trembling words at first, words seeking a re-entry into the dream world. Words looking for completion. And then anger, as her mind sorted out the scene in front of her. He was doing just what she had dreamed—and in her dream she had cried for more, even more. But the dream was shattered, and she was slowly rousing to rage. Not because of what he was actually doing, but rather because of what he had failed to do in her dream!

He mis-read the situation entirely, hunkering back on his heels and letting a mask slip over his face. The hawk mask. The predatory hawk. She gathered the sheet around her for protection, and slid as far away from him as the bed would allow.

'You have no right!' She stamped the words out one at a time, coldly, arraying them like little soldiers marching to battle.

'No,' he sighed. 'I—there aren't any excuses. I looked in to see if you were all right, and I saw you. That's something no ordinary man could resist. And that's all I am. An ordinary man. I suppose you would like me to say I'm sorry?'

'Not if you don't mean it.' She tried to encapsulate the words in ice, but failed. There was a tremor in her voice that she could not control. There was something about this troubled man that was growing on her. Some subtle thing she could not understand. Not grand passion. Not love. Just some indefinable—something.

'Well,' he sighed, struggling to his fee, 'then there's no use saying it, because I don't feel the least bit sorry, and I suspect I'd do it again the next chance I get!'

'Well, don't hold your breath waiting,' she snapped

at him. The dream had truly dissolved and things had returned to normal. She was still a refugee on a tiny island, afraid for her own safety and for her father's, locked into this man's schemes until the inspector left. And the last thing in the world you need, she told herself, is to fall into some crazy entanglement with this—arrogant man! How could it be possible that he fathered a lovely child like Josie? All of a sudden I feel a great deal of sympathy for his former wife, whoever she is!

His question came out of the clear blue sky. 'How old are you, Rose?'

'Twenty,' she snapped back at him, without giving it a thought.

'Ah! You do remember something!'

Oh Lord, shut your stupid mouth, she yelled at herself. Shut your stupid mouth!

'So you do remember something,' he insisted.

'Yes,' she said angrily, and defied him to pry another word out of her.

'So tell me what you remember.'

'I remember that I'm twenty,' she returned defiantly. And let me see you make something out of that, Mr Gendron!

He waited for a moment, hoping for some amplification. She sat up in the bed, holding the sheet up to her neck, defying him. 'All right,' he sighed. 'At least that's something.' He lifted a wrist to check his watch. 'Only twenty minutes until dinner time,' he commented. 'You'd better get dressed. This is our last performance with the Inspector. The ship will dock at seven tonight, and leave at four in the morning.'

She managed to be early, in fact. A girl whose wardrobe consists of three *muumuus*, four *pareaux*, and four sets of wrap-around skirts hardly finds a problem in dressing for dinner. For this night she chose another *muumuu*. When she walked out on to the veranda he was waiting for her with a tall cool glass in hand. He passed her the drink and slipped an arm around her waist.

'Look down there.' He gestured with his free hand. A few feet below the house Josie and Inspector Tihoni were deep in conference, *tête-à-tête*. The big man was sitting on a large tree stump. The little girl stood in front of him, her hands clasped behind her back. Even at this distance Rose and Giles could see that she had her fingers crossed. When the dinner gong rang the pair came slowly up the walk, seemignly content with their world. The Inspector smiled at them and walked by.

'I need to clean up,' he said. 'The records are somewhat dusty. Would you believe that the official papers have not been audited in fourteen years?' He hummed a little song as he went down the corridor towards the bathroom.

'What did he want,' Giles asked quickly.

'Nothing.' The little girl gave her father a hug. 'He asked me was I happy here with you and Mommy. So I told him sure I was. Who wouldn't be, I said. And then he said, you know, I have a family of my own. Six daughters, I have. And I said, that's nice. And then he said again about was I happy here, and I said of course I was, and wouldn't wanna live any place else 'cept with you and Dad.' A little hand stole out and trapped Rose's in a death grip. Rose squeezed a return promise that they both understood without words.

'Well what do you know,' Giles mused. 'Still suspicious. Troops, we need to put on a good show tonight, so we can send him off in a happy mood. Right?'

'Right,' Josie chimed in. 'Mommy? Right?'

'Oh—of course. Right.'

It didn't turn out to be a difficult problem. Sam Apuka appeared as an added guest, and Miri joined them at the table. The conversation was world-wide, and then localised.

'Yes,' Sam answered the Inspector's question. 'We grow here on Te Tuahine. Now we are eighty three people. Forty-four children and thirty-nine adults. The life is good. But we worry about the reef, you know. When France has need of us they blast a hole in the reef. It costs much money. Now Tahiti governs itself. Where comes the money to blast again? Already the reef grows, no? Even the local freighter, he worries to come in. What becomes of us when the reef closes?'

They all sat and stared at each other. Change the subject, Rose commanded herself. Be a real hostess. Turn them into some other line of thought. Quick! She took a deep breath, dived off the deep end, and —'Miri, when are you and Sam going to get married?'

Every adult at the table turned to stare at her. Miri turned her head away and giggled nervously—the sort of giggle that denotes embarrassment all around the Pacific basin. Somebody kicked Rose in the ankle under the table. It became stunningly obvious to her that she had managed to get both feet in her mouth with one sentence!

'Perhaps I could explain,' the Inspector offered. Since nobody else made an offer, Rose turned to him in desperation. His face was awash in strange expressions, as if he were carefully marshalling all the right words before he spoke.

'It is still the custom of the outer islands as in the old days,' the policeman started out cautiously. 'People marry to raise families, and boy children are most necessary, you understand.'

Feeling utterly stupid, Rose nodded her head.

'And so you must see that a man who wishes to raise a family would want to be—er—sure that he would have boy children, no?'

'It—it sounds plausible,' she stammered, wondering how deeply the basic Polynesian sex lecture was going to go. 'But there is a catch in it?'

'A delightful expression. Catch in it! American?' She nodded. 'So it is the custom that a girl should be able to demonstrate that—er—she can—ah—provide boy children before the marriage is arranged. You understand?'

'What!' All her beliefs were outraged, and she could not hold back. 'You mean to tell me that Miri has to——' Giles was signalling to her, gesturing to where Josie sat at the foot of the table, her little ears perked up so as not to miss a word. Oh Lord, Rose sighed to herself. Oh Lord! She struggled to regain control over her face, and sank back in her chair. The silence around her broke as everybody tried to introduce a new subject, all at the same time. Rose let it all wash over her. But she could not leave it lie; she had to worry the bone just one more time. 'Everybody knows,' she muttered under her breath, 'that the male determines the sex of the child!' Which earned her another warning kick on her ankle!

The dinner party broke up at nine o'clock. Josie was yawning madly, as was the Inspector. Sam and Miri seemed to be eating each other up with their eyes, and soon they made their excuses and went off to the village. In the distance they heard conch-shell trumpets announcing that the old supply ship had returned.

'That Apuka is a fine man,' the Inspector said as he rose from the table. 'He'll make a fine headman here. And you, Mr Gendron, Mrs Gendron——' he seemed to hesitate between the two names. 'You add something to the island. I will file a negative report about this case of kidnapping. There is clearly no truth in it. All the papers will be filed in our headquarters in Papeete. And by this time next year nobody will be able to find it, not even for the most inquisitive of American Consuls. So I say good night. In the early morning I go quietly, not to waken you. I wish you many sons.' He waved to them all and went off down the hall.

Giles put his arm around her waist. He's been doing

a lot of that lately, Rose thought. And it's not too unenjoyable, either. And then Josie came around from the other side of the table and butted her head into Rose's side.

'Tired, love?' she asked. The little girl nodded wearily.

'Did we do a good job, Daddy?' the child asked.

'Remarkably good,' he said softly. 'It couldn't be better. Just a few more hours now, and we'll all be away free and clear.' Rose noticed the inflection. *We'll all be*— as if they shared a conspiracy together. But it did sound— nice. Just a few more hours, and it would no longer be important what the Inspector remembered about Rose Harriet Lambert. She wrapped an arm around the pair standing on either side of her. It's really not difficult at all to think of myself as Rose Gendron! I'll think about his little con game tomorrow. When the sounds of the policeman moving around from bathroom to bedroom had stilled, she squeezed Josie's hand.

'First it's bed for you, love,' she whispered, 'And then me. Come on. You can shower in the morning.' The little attentions, the settling down, the little story, all filled a half-hour. When Josie was finally asleep Rose stood up and stretched. Lord, it had been a strange day, among strange people. What a crazy mix-up! She walked down to her own room, fumbling in the dark for the shorty nightgown she had made for herself. The moon was late in rising, and the tropical darkness had settled on everything. Moving around the bedroom she stumbled a couple of times. Those darn packages, she swore under her breath. I forgot to ask anybody about them, and they're all over the room! But in the end she managed to finish her own toilette, and tumbled into bed.

I'm beginning to live in this bed, she thought. I spent most of the morning here, part of the afternoon, and now here I go again. I don't think I can sleep, but I can—suddenly she was shaken out of her musings. Somebody had brushed the drapes aside at her door and had come into her room. 'Who is it,' she hissed, wary of waking the little girl next door.

'It's me,' he answered softly. 'Where the devil is my— damn, did they have to put all those packages in the middle of the floor!'

'Shh,' she retorted. 'Josie's asleep. What in the world are you doing in my room?' She could hear by the noise that he had found his way across the cluttered floor, and had settled into the chair by the bed. 'Well?'

'Well what?' One of his shoes clumped as it landed on the floor.

'What are you doing!' She could feel panic rising, blocking her throat.

'I'm getting undressed. What the devil do you think I'm doing?'

'You can't undress here. You must be out of your ever-loving mind! Get out of here. Go back to your own room!'

'Think!' he snorted. The other shoe dropped to the floor.

'"Think?' she hissed. 'If you don't get out of here I'm going to scream the house down!'

'Go ahead,' he said under his breath. There seemed to be two or three other words involved there, but Rose decided that she just didn't want to hear them.

'Why—why are you doing this to me,' she sighed. The tears edged closer to her eyelashes. 'Why did you——'

'Think,' he repeated. 'We've got three bedrooms. Josie has one, the Inspector has one, and that leaves this one to be shared between my wife and I. My wife certainly won't mind sharing a room with me, will she?'

'What kind of logic is that,' she snarled at him. 'I told you before I didn't want you to lay a hand on me until——'

'Oh just shut up and move over, Rose,' he snapped. 'The bed is wide enough for four of us to sleep here. There's no way of avoiding this. Mr and Mrs Gendron spent a quiet night in the connubial nest, and the Inspector goes home to Tahiti without a care in the world, right?' The bed sank and rocked as he stretched out beside her. It was too dark to see what he was wearing, and she was driven by a need to know. She stretched out one tentative finger in his general direction. Somehow he sensed it was coming, and seized it in one of his big paws. She tried to pull away, but he moved her hand inexorably forward, until the fingertip touched his upper thigh. Nothing, her finger signalled. That's what he wears in bed. Nothing!

'For heaven's sake,' he muttered into her ear. 'I don't plan any great rape scenes, Rose. Close your eyes, there's a good girl, and let's see if at least one of us can get some sleep before morning.'

She snatched her finger away. Its tip was burning, burning. She moved it to her mouth and sucked on it, trying to control her panic. He shifted in the bed a couple of times, rocking her, sending shivers up her spine. In all her life she had never shared a bed with anyone, never mind a full-grown virile male! And how come you think about him that way, Rose, her conscience asked. A full-grown virile male, indeed! She held her breath so she could listen to his. He seemed to be exhaling more slowly, as if he were asleep. She extended her finger again—just to be sure he was asleep, of course. He was much closer. Too much closer! Her finger touched gently on his chest, felt the warmth of it, and the pulsing life within. Damn! She pulled the finger back, turned on her side with her back to him, and did her best to compose herself. It wasn't easy. Counting sheep didn't help. But counting *tiki* statues did. Row after row of little stone statues she counted, manoeuvred, re-arranged. They all looked like Pele. He wants you. That's what her dream on Pele's *maere* had told her. He wants you. Eventually, if you count high enough, you discover that he wants you. How much higher do I have to count before he *gets* me? And with that thought wrapped around her she dozed off.

Sometime late in the night, long after the Inspector had stolen quietly away to the ship, a rain storm swept down on the island, cleaning the air and adding depth to the perfume of the night flowers. In typical tropical style it poured an inch of rain down in an hour. The huge drops battered at the corrugated roof of the house, and the crescendo of smashing bashing water startled Rose into half-wakefulness. Instinctively she recoiled and found herself hard up against his frame. He reacted. Two arms came around her, pulling her closer. There was an instantaneous feeling of— protection, comfort. She relaxed against him, halfway back in her dream, enjoying the soothing motion of his hand on her stomach.

'I——' she started to say.

'Don't talk,' he whispered in her ear. 'Don't talk. I know. Everything's all right.' There was a hypnotic spell in that deep voice of his. He continued talking, saying nothing, and gradually she fell under the spell of it all. When his hand moved upward from her stomach to the mound of her breast it all seemed—proper. She made no protest. But when he walked his fingers up to the roseate tip of that lovely mountain the world seemed to jump all around her. For the first time in her life she felt a wicked response, a driving flaming spark that ignited all the passions that a woman possesses. He's my husband, she told herself fiercely. He's my husband. And knowing the lie, it was still excuse enough to overcome her doubts. She gasped and turned towards him, opening her eyes for the first time.

He loomed over her, a huge dark shadow in a darker

room. She could feel the strength of him, the maleness of him, as he moved closer. His lips brushed hers. A tender touch, warm, moist, pleasant. And then they returned, at the same time that his hand stroked her silken flank. The pressure of his lips became more urgent, more demanding. She started to say something, and his tongue slipped past her guard. And her world blew up!

She snatched at him madly, winding her arms around his bare shoulders, pressing herself hard to conform to his contours. He tantalised her mouth for an endless time, and then slipped away from her lips, nibbled at her ear, the softness of her throat. And then he moved down to where her swollen breasts waited to receive him. She squirmed against him frantically, not knowing what else to do. Her fingernails left marks on his back, red striations that matched the fever in her brain. Someone was moaning in a soft contralto voice.

He fumbled briefly with her nightgown, then one of his huge hands seized it at the neckline and tore it straight down. She had the crazy urge to get closer to him, to feel the hardness of him all over her soft skin. Wildly she struggled to free her arms from the remnants of her gown. His hands played havoc with her, running up and down her back, across her buttocks, down her thighs. He broke her stranglehold around his neck, turning her over flat on her back. His hands moved again, down the little mound of her stomach, into the area where no one had ever been before. She could feel the scream of pleasure building up in her as he caressed just the right spots. 'Giles,' she whispered fiercely at him. 'Do it! Do it now!'

There was no time for thought no room for conversation, no place for explanation. Do it, her mind kept screaming. Do it now! He rolled over on top of her. She welcomed his weight, as her tensions mounted higher and higher. He brushed her legs apart and poised himself, gone beyond control beyond stopping. She pulled and tugged at him, urging him closer, into the final union. And the pain struck her. Slight, transitory, but a warning none the less.

It was enough to bring her back to reality. Her whole mind and body froze in position, interrupting the delicious rhythm that had sent her into mindless ecstasy. 'No,' she muttered, and then louder, 'No!'

He was too far gone to stop, although he recognised that his partner was no longer with him. In one wild surge he reached his peak, and collapsed on top of her. And it was only then that he recognised the meaning of the frail barrier he had destroyed. She lay there beneath him, trembling, suddenly cold. Tears ran down her cheeks.

'Rose?' Half doubtfully, half apologetic.

'Damn you! Damn you! You had no right!' Her voice was a fierce hissing whisper, filled with all the remorse of years. The pain had quickly disappeared, but the memory of it hung over her head. 'You had no right,' she hissed at him.

'I thought you gave me the right, Rose,' he returned hoarsely, unbelieving. 'You came to me, I didn't come to you! I thought that was what you wanted.'

'Well you thought wrong, damn you! I didn't invite you. It was the storm. It—it frightened me!'

Her mind struggled, seeking an excuse for herself. He had no right! The storm—and—I could have stopped him! Why didn't I? I've never had any trouble stopping all the other grapplers. Was it because he told me I was his wife? He almost had me believing it! He *did* have me believing it. It has to be *his* fault. I couldn't stand it if it were *my* fault. I'd just—just break up in little pieces. All those years. Saving myself for this? It *has* to be his fault. Who could have expected that it would hurt so much? My God, what has he done to me!

Her hands pushed ineffectively at him, until finally he roused and rolled to the edge of the bed. What in God's name have I done to her, he thought. Not only a sweet lovable kid, but a virgin to boot. I've really done it this time. But I—I thought that was what she wanted! Why am I trying to excuse myself now! Why didn't she find it as good as I did?

'I'm—terribly sorry, Rose,' he whispered. 'I didn't mean it to happen. It was just—one of those things. I really thought you wanted it!'

'Yes,' she hissed at him. 'Just one of those things. A one-night stand. I hope you enjoyed yourself, because *I* certainly didn't. God, what have you done to me!'

'I didn't realise—I just couldn't stop, Rose. What can I do to make you see how sorry I am. I'll do anything!'

'I'll bet you will.' Her voice was as cold as an Arctic mountaintop. She drew away from him, sitting up against the headboard on the far side of the bed. 'I was your wife, you said. And Josie was my daughter. Sure! What other lies did you tell me?' It isn't true, her conscience complained. You know it isn't true!

'I'll do anything, Rose. Ask me anything.' She could hear the agony in his voice, and it pleased her to know he was suffering.

'Fine,' she grated between her teeth. 'Make me a virgin again.'

He snatched at his shirt and shorts and stomped out to the veranda, snarling both at himself and at her. 'I don't do miracles,' he muttered, banging his fist into the bamboo pillar of the veranda.

Straight ahead of him, to the east, the sun was a thin line of light against the horizon. The sea breeze blew in at him, laden with fresh-washed air. In the distance gulls were diving inside the reef. Near at hand the wind rustled through the paper-thin leaves of the bougainvillaea. Behind him, through the window he could hear her softly weeping. 'I'm a cross between Hitler and Attilia the Hun,' he muttered as he searched his pockets for a cigarette. The weight that his conscience saddled on him was heavier than any burden he had ever carried in his life.

CHAPTER SEVEN

SHE sat in the dim corner of her bedroom for half the morning, huddled in a chair near the window, completely covered from head to toe in the largest *muumuu* she could find. Time after time she tried to think logically, and was unable to do so. Time after time she relived those few minutes in the night that had so completely changed her life. 'If only I had stopped him,' she muttered to herself. I could have stopped him. Couldn't I? I never meant it to be this way. I always dreamed of—a man who loved me. There was no love last night, not on either side. Animals, both of us. But it was his fault. If he hadn't lied and cheated, if he hadn't forced himself into my bed, none of it would have happened. So it *is* his fault. Damn the man!

Miri brushed the door drapes aside and came in, stopping suddenly when she saw Rose huddled in the corner. *'Aue.'* she exclaimed softly. 'I think you are at the beach, Mrs. I come back later and——'

'No,' Rose sighed. 'Go ahead with whatever you have to do.'

'You don't even open the presents?'

'What presents?'

'Here.' Miri pointed to the half dozen packages littering the room. 'You don't even open? He spends many days to look in catalogue. Look here.' She picked up one of the smaller bundles and opened it, laying its contents out on the bed. 'There. What you think?'

It was an exciting collection of European clothing. Everything from day dresses, slips, underwear, daring bikinis. Miri hugged one of the sheer little blouses to her cheek. 'Lovely,' she chanted. 'You like?'

'No, I don't like,' Rose snapped. 'Get them out of here. All of them. Right now, Miri. Get them out of here!' Her voice rose to a crescendo of loathing that could be heard throughout the house.

'You no like? I——'

'Get them out of here,' she snarled. 'Now!'

The other woman stared at her with wide eyes, and then began to collect the packages in her arms. 'You think he will——'

'I don't give a damn what he will,' Rose shouted. The Polynesian girl shrugged her shoulders and went out with her arms loaded. A few minutes later Giles tapped on the doorframe and walked in. One all-encompassing look was all he needed.

'You're acting like a child,' he said gruffly. 'The clothes were ordered a week ago. You——'

'I don't want anything from you,' she told him through clenched teeth. 'I don't want *anything* from you. All I want is to get out of here. And if you ever touch me again, so help me God I'll kill you!'

'So, you're convinced it was all my fault, are you? You had nothing to do with it?'

'Yes,' she snarled at him. 'Get out of here. Surely I can have some place to myself. I don't think I've ever hated a man as much as I hate you. Get out of here!'

'Be honest with yourself. It wasn't rape, you know.'

'It was,' she shrilled at him. 'Lies and deceit, and then brute force. Oh it was rape all right. I was your wife, remember? Mother of your daughter? Hah!' She wrapped her arms around herself and rocked back and forth miserably in the chair.

'All right,' he sighed. 'And now we have to talk about what happens next. After we're married, I thought we would——'

'Married,' she screamed, and struggled to her feet, threatening him with both fists. Now what the hell, he asked himself. Thank God I sent Josie off to the village with Miri!

'After last night, the least I can do is marry you,' he offered stiffly. 'After all, you might very well be pregnant, you know. It seems the only sensible thing to do, for us to get married.'

'Sensible!' she screamed.

'Yes, sensible,' he said, struggling to keep calm. It's like talking to a volcano, he told himself as he watched her shake and shiver in her rage. 'I need a wife, and you need a husband. Especially if you should be pregnant. Under the circumstances, I——'

She had simmered down, but only slightly. 'I wouldn't marry you if you were the last man on earth,' she shouted, pounding out the rhythm of each word by thumping a fist into her open palm. 'You are undoubtedly the most arrogant, arrant man I've ever known. Do you really think I would let you take over my life after what you did to me last night?'

He lost control. 'Well, I'm not all that keen about marrying you, either,' he snapped. 'But we have to. As it happens——'

'Forget it,' she interrupted. 'It's not going to happen, damn you. And as for being pregnant, I thought it was the island custom to see if I could produce a boy before you offered marriage! Damn all you men. Now you let me tell you something, Mr Know-It-All Gendron. The only thing I want from you is a way off this island. And quickly.'

He stared at her, non-plussed. It had taken a whole morning of musing for him to come up with the idea of marriage. And here she was turning it down in anger, insulted. A perfectly legitimate offer that an awful lot of women would grab at!

'I could make you a very good husband,' he told her self-righteously.

'You haven't proven it yet,' she snarled back at him. 'It takes two to tango. You're already a one-time loser.

Why wouldn't Helen want to keep you on? Because you're such a good husband? Hah!'

'That's hitting below the belt,' he objected.

'I just hope so,' she snapped at him. 'This is supposed to be a serious discussion. I don't have time for little jokes, like *Rose is going to marry Giles*. Now, how soon can I get off this island?'

He leaned back in his chair, fumbling around in his mind. No matter how he added it up, it still came out the same way. She *had* to marry him. And it wasn't only the matter of easing my own conscience. Josie is the main problem. I have to do something about Josie, and quickly. Why didn't I notice that the child is growing up? She acts more and more like a native girl every day, and her English is so bad that—wow. She needs a mother, that one. One whom she respects, and even—loves? Rose Harriet just fits the bill. And then there's me. But his usually facile mind refused to wrestle with *that* problem.

He fingered the newspaper clipping in the pocket of his shorts. The one he had cut out of the newspapers that arrived with the supply boat. She needs us as badly as we need her. Now why in hell can't she *see* that! What we—all three of us—need is time. Time enough for Josie to settle down. Time enough for me to paper over that massive mistake I made last night. Hey, as far as she's concerned, I'm the good guys. So I'm not in love with her—relationships have been built without love by many a couple. I'll do it. After you've been accused of rape, blackmail is hardly a terrible crime!

'I'm afraid that's impossible,' he told her. 'There's no way off this island until the next supply boat comes. That will be, oh let me see now—three months from now. December. Close on Christmas, I suppose.' And try that one on for size, little lady! He watched the sudden flare in her eyes.

'You mean I have to wait around here for three months?' Her face reflected her astonishment.

'Three months? Never!'

'I thought you never said never,' he chuckled. 'But that's correct. Three months until the next boat. You could swim, of course. Maupiti is just six miles over that way.' He waved to the north. 'Now that's civilization. They have air service to Tahiti three times a week. Most weeks, that is.'

'Six miles? That's not very far. I'll bet I could get one of the fishermen to take me over there.'

'No you don't, Rose Gendron. Don't get the villagers mixed up in our problems!'

'I'm not Rose Gendron, damn you. I'm not your wife. I never was your wife, was I! You proved that last night, you—you monster. I hope the Inspector comes back so I can tell him about you and your daughter!'

'That's blackmail, Rose. Out and out blackmail!'

'And you deserve it. Every bit of it!'

He stood up, towering over her. He's doing that on purpose, she told herself. Trying to intimidate me. Monster!

'You seem to recall a great deal these days, Rose,' he said amiably. 'You're twenty, you're not my wife, you hate me—what else do you remember, Rose?'

She was too angry to control her tongue. 'Everything!' she snarled at him.

'Everything?' He cocked one eyebrow at her.

'Yes, damn you,' she shouted at him. 'You thought you were so damn smart, didn't you? Play the little lady for a sucker? Hah! Let me tell you something, you conniving—you—you. I never did have amnesia. Not at all! So there!'

It was all out before she could stop herself. And then, shivering with anger, she had to stand there while he bent over almost double, laughing until the tears came to his eyes. Just once, she thought—just once I'd like to be a man. I'd beat him up something fierce! I'd—'Why are you laughing?'

'Rose, that's funny,' he gurgled. 'While we were busy conning you, you were busy conning us! Now that's funny!'

'Well I don't see the humour of it,' she said coldly. 'I was scared half to death.'

'And you know what makes it even funnier,' he chuckled. 'The rape scene. So it was rape because I told you you were my wife. Naughty naughty, Rose!' He shook an admonitory finger at her and broke out in uninhibited laughter again. She stamped her little foot in anger, unable to free herself from the sudden cold fear that struck her.

'Sit down, Rose.' He forced her into a chair. She perched nervously on its edge, her back straight, feet flat on the floor, heels together. Her fingers nervously wrestled with each other in her lap.

'So tell me about Rose Lambert,' he said softly.

'I don't remember any Rose Lambert,' she muttered.

'Then you've got a very strange memory,' he snorted. 'Look at this.' The crumpled paper he handed her was from the front page of the Papeete newspaper. She unfolded it and stared.

HAVE YOU SEEN THIS WOMAN, the headline said. Beneath it was a distorted picture of Rose Lambert, on her fourteenth birthday, with her hair in two pigtails, and her undeveloped face almost unrecognisable. It's the picture Papa always carried in his wallet, she told herself. So they *must* have Papa. Or perhaps just his wallet? She brushed the thought aside, and read on.

'Police in the islands are searching for ROSE HARRIET LAMBERT, the daughter of one of the principles in the investigation of the fire and embezzlement at the Banque de Pacifique early in September. During that crime two million francs in gold, currency, and securities were stolen, and the building torched to hide the evidence. Miss Lambert was last seen aboard the yacht *Southwinds*, during the typhoon of September 7th. Miss Lambert stands five feet four inches, with long blonde hair and green eyes. A reward is offered for information.'

She handed it back to him, on the defensive. The slight breeze that sometimes wanders through in the heat of mid-morning wrestled with her hair, blowing it into a clever mask across her features. 'No, I don't remember any Rose Lambert,' she muttered.

He laughed again. A short barking laugh, with a triumphant ring to it. 'Despite all the sudden truths,' he said, 'you and I have a great need of each other. I need someone to look after Josie for the next three months. Someone who can love her and teach her how to be a woman. If you agree to do that, I guarantee to get you out of the islands—to anywhere. Samoa, New Zealand, the States. Anywhere. And along with that I can promise you a stake to start life over again. What do you say to that?'

'What the devil did you suppose I would say,' she shouted at him. 'No! I intend to find some way off this island, and the sooner the better!'

'Why now that's too bad,' he mourned, plainly not meaning it. He leaned over closer to her and, in a conspiratorial whisper said, 'Just remember, the first minute that I find you gone from the island, Rose, I will radio the Police that Rose Lambert is on her way to Maupiti. There's a reward, Rose! And think what sort of welcome you'll get when you come ashore!'

'Why you—you——' She was entirely out of words bad enough to be used on him, and he was laughing again. She took six deep breaths and fought to control her temper. 'That's pure blackmail,' she squeaked at him. 'Blackmail!'

'Isn't it though,' he laughed. 'Bargain?'

She jumped up, and immediately regretted the move. He was much closer. And somehow much bigger. She clenched both fists so tightly that her nails bit into the palms of her hands. She shook and trembled in her anger, and her fists wavered. But it was thought, not anger that she required to elude his trap, she told herself. She walked away from him, stamping her feet down hard to steady her nerves. Up and down the restricted space she stomped. He moved back out of the way and let her pace.

It was fear of the unknown that held her in thrall. What has happened to Papa? If the police have *him*, why would they want me? Any step I take, any word I speak, might harm poor Papa. Information. I've got to get more information. *Somebody* knows! The Inspector certainly, but he's gone. There has to be some other source of news. And until I get more information I have to—to give in to this—monster. I have to! Mind made up, she ground to a halt in front of him.

She stared at the third button on his shirt, refusing to meet his eyes. Her hands were clasped behind her back. He needn't know *everything* I think, she told herself fiercely.

'All right,' she grumbled. 'It's a bargain.'

'And very graciously said,' he chuckled. 'So, for three more months you will be Mrs Rose Gendron, and will instil some discipline in my daughter, and teach her how to grow up.'

'Hey, wait. I didn't agree to be any Mrs Gendron. That's not in the cards.'

'All or nothing, Rose,' he said solemnly. 'All or nothing.'

'Oh—I—damn you. You'd better not touch me, do you hear!'

'I hear, love. And I swear I won't ever touch you—damn, there's that word again. I swear that I won't hardly ever touch you, except for when you ask me to.'

'And *that* will be a cold day in summer,' she huffed.

'And I'll expect you to dress up to the name,' he

continued, 'so you will accept the clothes I bought for you. Right?'

'Damn you,' she muttered, and turned away. There's a difference between accepting and wearing, she told herself.

'Hey, that's no way for a lady to talk,' he added. 'Here comes your daughter. Switch heads, Rose darling. You are now officially my wife again.'

'Damn you,' she muttered again. It was all the words she could muster.

Josie was all chatter that night. Miri had taken her through the village, re-introducing her to the children, presenting her to the elders.

'And that boy Terri,' she chattered. 'He's my age, or something, and he has his own outrigger canoe, Mommy. He took me out on the bay and we fished. I didn't catch nothin', but he said that was okay, 'cause girls aren't supposed to fish anyways—that's man's work.'

And that is the first link in your set of chains, Rose whispered under her breath as she scrubbed the little girl's back under the shower. The first step is to convince you that men can do things better than women, and that's the beginning of female subjugation. Damn men!

'What did you say, Mommy?'

'Nothing. Nothing, dear. You got a good burn on your shoulders. The next time you go out for the day you must remember to put some sunscreen on.'

'How come? Terri doesn't wear sunscreen.'

'No, and he doesn't have your European skin either, love. You just remember that.'

'Why?'

Rose laughed at herself. A sudden flashback had pictured her in the bathroom with *her* mother, having the same sort of argument. 'Because I said so, that's why.' And waited for the argument that never came.

'Oh.' Josie said. And that was the end of that subject.

She went tiredly to bed, but still had something on her mind. 'What Daddy bought you. Are you going to wear that stuff?'

'I don't know, love. Maybe we can make it into something for you to wear. We'll make a lady out of you yet!'

'I don't wanna be a lady,' the child murmered sleepily. 'I just wanna learn to be a good bow paddler.'

Rose had the luxury of coffee on the veranda when Josie finally dropped off. 'We can have coffee for maybe four, five weeks after the boat come,' Miri explained. 'Coffee and flour and green vegetables. Except he order something this time I don't know. Is called dehydrated potatoes. Nobody in kitchen knows what to do with potatoes.'

'I'll show you tomorrow,' Rose assured her. 'Leave the coffee pot, Miri. I feel like going on a binge.'

'*Aue*,' the other woman laughed. 'Better you drink *kaava*. Coffee drive you mad in moonlight. I hear somebody say that. I leave mug for Mister. He don't like cup.'

Live and learn, Rose sighed. Mister don't like cup! She stuck her tongue out at the open sky and poured herself a steaming black cupful—even spilling a little into the saucer as a sort of libation. She leaned back deep in the lounge chair and sipped and watched. The Southern Cross, deep in the sky. Venus, star of evening, sparkling bright—and far away. Sirius, the watch-star of the islands. All the panoply of heaven circled above her and intersticed her dream. Was it only a day ago that the world had been so shaken—her world? Was it only a night ago when she was forced over the border into womanhood? C'mon, her short-tempered conscience snapped at her, he didn't have to push very hard, did he? And then silently he was there.

'I smelled the brew,' he said. She leaned forward and filled the mug.

'Black? We have some powdered milk and lots of sugar, but I told Miri to leave it in the kitchen.'

'And a good thing,' he commented. 'We'd have all the insects within five miles charging up the stairs. Black is fine.' He settled into the other lounge chair. 'Lord, this is good. It's a pleasure to be able to relax again.' He stretched out, his long legs over-reaching the length of the lounger. They sat quietly.

'You've been working hard?' she asked. It was advanced casually, but she meant if for a flag of truce. There was no way her mind could sustain a steady hatred, with all burners going. And three months was a long time to get through.

'Yes,' he returned quietly. 'I've hit a snag.'

'Want to tell me about it?'

'Are you sure you want to hear?'

'Of course. I wouldn't ask if I didn't want to hear.'

He gulped down his coffee and refilled the mug, sitting up to face her as he did. In the darkness she could see only his outline, and the gleam of his teeth. So he's smiling, she thought—or getting ready to bite me?

'We have to make a killing with this book,' he began. 'I guess you realise that my former wife Helen just eats up our income with alimony payments. So I have to strike it big. Now usually I go for a straight adventure story. But to make this one movie-quality, I've got to add some sexy scenes. It's a must. Both my publisher and my agent say the same thing.'

'And?'

'And the *femme fatale* is just running away from me. I can't seem to meld her into the main theme.'

'Why don't you tell me about her?'

'All right. Why not.' He settled himself back in his chair again and began from the beginning, describing the plot, the main characters, and finally the woman. He talked for almost an hour, and very suddenly stopped in mid-sentence. She looked over at him. She had been half-listening, half-dreaming. He was running his hands through his hair. 'Damn! Of course!' he half shouted. 'That's why it won't come out even. I've got it now. Thanks, Rose! You certainly straightened me out in a hurry!' He jumped up and ran for his workroom.

'Yes, glad I could help,' she called after him. And then in a lower murmur, 'What the devil did I do to help? I never even said a word! Besides, it's a crazy plot. No self-respecting woman would act like that, ever. Well, hardly ever.'

But her coffee tasted sweeter, stronger, bolder when she went back to it, even though the entire cupful was cold. She looked around cautiously, and then laughed at herself. There was no need for caution. Josie was asleep. Giles was chained to his typewriter. Miri and the girls had all gone home. Giggling at herself, she leaned over the edge of the veranda and emptied her cup on to the ground. Then, hesitantly, she reached for his mug, filled it up, and leaned back to enjoy the flavour.

CHAPTER EIGHT

THE days that followed settled into a slow routine. An early morning swim, followed by breakfast. Lessons with Josie until the noonday heat brought everything to a halt. Naps for all. And then a time for exploring, usually spent with the child. Giles worked away, pounding the typewriter as if it were a mortal enemy. And then, a month after the freighter had sailed, Rose made a momentous discovery.

She had left Josie to struggle with a quiz on earth sciences, and walked down the hall to the bathroom. The door of his workroom was open. She stopped. The room was empty. Curiosity carried her across the threshold. Manuscript pages were piled helter-skelter. It was too much for her neat soul.

She leaned over and picked up a double handful of papers from the floor, shuffled them into some order, and searched the desk for someplace to put them. And immediately lost track of her original idea.

Squarely in the middle of the desk, in the only orderly area, was a small pile of envelopes, some unopened. Mail! For years she had sorted and classified her father's mail, and her fingers moved automatically to sort through this pile. Two letters from Papeete. Bills, apparently, with the little glassene slot to show an address. One letter from San Francisco in a bold heavy hand. One from New York, in a light feminine scribble. That last one was unopened. She checked the return address, just for curiosity's sake, she told herself. 'Helen Morley Gendron.' So his first wife still corresponded, and still used *his* name. She felt a little touch of

131

annoyance at that, and dropped the envelopes back on the desk.

Something was nagging at her mind. She picked up the envelopes again, and sorted out the two bills from Tahiti. Something about them. What? She looked them over carefully, tapping one of them against her front teeth in an old familiar habit. Trying to start up her thinking motor, her father always said. What was it?

She scanned the top envelope again. Just a bill, from Dupont y Freres, Victuallers. Nothing unusual, except— the cancellation! Six days old! Six days ago the envelope in her hand had been processed through the main Post Office at Papeete. Six days ago! And what was it he had said? 'There's no way off this island until the freighter comes back, in three months?' Then how in God's green world had this letter come all the way from Tahiti in six days?

She could feel the wild surge of excitement run up her spine. Information, wasn't that what she needed? And here was her first clue. In some manner, mail had been delivered to this island within the last six days. Oh, that horribly monstrous man! There *was* a way! He had trapped her into his blackmail arrangement because she thought there was no way off the island. And he had lied to her! Again! She slammed the letters back down on the desk and then, for good measure, picked up the neat pile of manuscript pages she had assembled. It improved her feelings immeasurably to toss the pages up in the air and let them find their own home.

'That's a big help, thank you!' He was leaning against the doorjamb, watching her with those predatory eyes.

'It's no more than you deserve,' she snapped at him. 'It's——' She clapped her hand over her mouth. Don't tell him about the mail, she screamed at herself. It can only help *you* if he doesn't know that you know! Shut up, little fool!

'I—I was walking by and thought I heard the wind blowing your papers around, so I came in to——'

'Yeah, wind,' he grunted. 'I saw you helping me out.' He stalked across the room and planted himself firmly in front of her. 'Why not try the truth for a change!'

'Why me,' she snarled. 'That's a commodity that doesn't get a great deal of use around here.'

'Why?'

'All right,' she shrilled at him. 'I'll tell you the truth! I was looking desperately for a way to get off this island. And I didn't find anything. And that made me mad. You deserved it!'

'You bet,' he sighed. 'Everything's my fault, right? I deserve every little torment your tiny mind can think up?'

'Right!' She tried to walk around him, indignation burning in her eyes. One of his arms stopped her.

'Whoa up,' he grunted. 'I wouldn't want you to think you can get away with everything in the world, Mrs Gendron. You deserve this.'

His hands swept into her armpits and hauled her up into the air until her nose was exactly at his level. 'Put me down you overgrown——' she roared.

'Run out of words?' He laughed. She kicked at him, remembering too late that she was barefoot. Her sensitive toes stung as they bounced off his hard kneecap.

'Put me down, you arrogant monster!'

'That's better,' he offered. And then the hands slowly levered her towards him until nose touched nose. She ducked her head, only to find his mouth had found its mark on hers. She squirmed against him, kicking, pummelling. But every move she made served only to exaggerate the pressure of his lips. Out of breath, she gave up, hanging in his arms like a big rag doll. And then a flash of fire, a spark of no mean dimension flashed between them. She found herself drowning,

drowning. Dissolving out of herself, invading the separate atoms of his being, being re-forged there as a part of him. The world rotated crazily. She closed her eyes to steady herself, only to find that the darkness accentuated the passions, the fears, the flaming pleasures that were running riot within her. Just when it seemed she could live no further, refuse him nothing, he set her aside and dropped her to the floor.

She leaned against him for support, struggling to regain control of her errant body. He kept a steadying hand at her back. She swallowed, gulped for fresh air, and peered up at him through her dishevelled hair He was guardedly watching. Attentive, she thought bleakly—perhaps even a little apprehensive? She forced herself away from him, even though her feet provided only feeble support. 'Damn you,' she muttered. He folded his arms across his chest and waited.

'Damn you,' she screamed, and ran for the door, tears streaming down her face. She stopped in the doorway and turned around. He held up both hands, palms facing her.

'I know,' he said wearily. 'Don't you ever touch me again!'

'Yes,' she sniffled. And then more determinedly, 'Yes, damn you!'

'And it seemed like such a good idea at the time!' She shook her hair back out of her eyes and searched his face for the sarcasm that wasn't there. Too overcome by emotions to make another response she whirled and ran for the bathroom. When she came back out ten minutes later and ghosted by the door of the workroom, he was sitting at the desk, his head down on his arms. Warily, she made for the veranda.

'You got something in your eye?' The little girl was sitting back in her chair, the completed test form in front of her.

'Yes,' Rose acknowledged glumly. 'Your father.' She

regretted the words immediately. There's no need to include the child in your feud with her father, she stormed at herself. Cut it out!

'You got Daddy in your eye?'

'No—well, yes. I had something in my eye, and your father tried to get it out for me. Have you finished the lesson?'

'Yes ma'am.' Two impudent little hands folded themselves angelically on the edge of the table. Suspicion reigned.

'No cheating?'

'Nope.'

'You didn't look at the back of my book for the answers?'

'Oh, is that where they are?'

'Don't be a smarty. Let me see the paper.'

Correction and discussions took them up to lunch time. They were alone at the table. Giles had disappeared somewhere, Miri told them.

After lunch she enticed the little girl to forego her nap. 'I've got a special class lined up for you,' she teased. Happy to be out in the air, Josie held her hand and skipped all the way down to the edge of the village. The *tahu'a* was waiting for them there, at the door of the largest hut in the area. He led them down to the shore. The tide was at its lowest ebb.

'Geography,' Rose announced, 'and History too.' The child laughed and looked around. The old man picked up a stick and began to draw. As he made his little symbols he sang them an explanation.

'Why it's the story of the Great Canoes,' Josie murmured as she watched him designate islands and currents and the history of the great Polynesian migration.

'From out of Havaki,' the old man chanted, and stopped. 'The old Havaki—the original land, no? From out of Havaki came the great canoes.' And the story went on. How the first boats had followed the birds and the wind and stars, found islands under their stationary clouds, avoided the lands of the Melanesians, and finally settled in Samoa and Tahiti. And then the second wave, coming out of Samoa and Tahiti, stretching east towards Easter Island, north towards Hawaii, south to New Zealand, and back westward again, into the island left behind them in the first migration. Bringing their *tapuus* and their gods with them. Tangora, master of the seas; Ora, the man-slayer; Tane the god of the land, and the wild mad Pele, she of volcanoes.

The little girl watched, entranced, as the Pacific islands were named and charted before her eyes. Rose felt somewhat removed and watched casually at first, but was soon drawn into the tale. Until it came to a stop. Two other men of the village came up and said something to the *tahu'a*. The old man reflected for a moment before he answered. They did not like what they heard, but they went away. The woman and child stared at the diagram in the sand.

'What did they say?' Rose queried. She knew it was something about the lesson, and she hated to think that the old man might be in some trouble because of her. He laughed at her discomfort.

'They say, *why teach the Great Path to a little girl.*'

'Is that bad? I suppose—it's something that only men should know?'

The old man laughed again, and used his stick to make a sign in the sand, almost a copy of the Egyptian Tau cross. 'I tell them,' he continued in his dry voice, 'I don't teach the child. I do what Pele tells me. I teach the woman. You come again another day?'

'I—Josie?'

'You bet, Mommy. If that's what geography is, I like it. How come my book only says what ar the fifty states, and who was George Washington?'

'Well,' she stalled, 'there are different kinds of

history. And we have to bring you up as an American, you know.'

'Okay.' Rose was surprised again at the lack of argument. 'We can come soon?' the little girl queried. The *tahu'a* ruffled her hair with his big hand. '*Ea*,' he said. 'You and your mother. *Au revoir!*' He unfolded his frame gracefully and walked away.

'Shall we go home now?' the child asked. And tugged at her *pareau* when Rose didn't answer.

'What? I'm sorry, dear. I was looking for someone. What did you say?'

'I said why don't we go swimming,' the little girl laughed. 'There's Terri out there waving at me.'

Rose held up a hand over her eyes to shade them. The Polynesian boy looked just like all the village boys. Just the sort of person Giles would rather Josie not associate with regularly. Oh hell, she told herself, I'm the girl's mother. She gave the child a little shoulder-shove in the right direction. 'Go play with him,' she chuckled. 'I've got to see someone myself.'

She watched for a minute as Josie ran down the beach towards the other children. She felt no qualms at letting her go. There were ten to fifteen adults on various sections of the sand, and Rose had learned something early on. In Tahiti and the islands one never watched one's own child—one watched *everybody's* child. There were at least ten surrogate mothers out there now who were registering Josie in their care. And if nobody came back for her there would be a happy squabble among the ten as to which one would take her home for the night. And keep her for a week if need be.

Rose was smiling as she sauntered down the beach towards her quarry. Sam Apuka was working slowly but steadily on an overturned boat, pounding sennet into the seams. He looked up as she greeted him, and stopped to wipe his forehead.

'*Iorana*,' he offered, and waited for her to speak.

'I don't want to interrupt,' she said hesitantly. He shrugged, and waved a hand at the boat.

'No interruption,' he laughed. 'This canoe leaks when I go away, four—five years ago. Now I am back a month, it still leaks. I don't fix it today, maybe it leaks next week. Not important. Good you bring big hat. Sun is no good for *popa'a* heads.'

'I just wanted to take a minute,' she said, crossing her fingers behind her. 'Mr Gendron, he—he thinks we should have five letters, and we only have four.'

'*Aue*,' the big man said. 'I don't count. Maybe one is still in Maupiti, no? We go tomorrow. I will remember.'

'Oh, you're going tomorrow? I didn't realize it would be so soon.'

Apuka looked at her indulgently. The sort of look reserved for children, the mentally deficient, and curious young women. 'We go every week on Friday,' he said. 'The airplane brings from Tahiti in the morning. We pick up at noon, come back by nightfall. If it don't storm!'

And there, Mr Giles Gendron, she told herself. I've got you! There's a boat that goes out of here once a week, and makes an air connection! Well, Mr Gendron?

'You make funny faces,' Sam chuckled. 'Eh, we have big dance tonight. Dance *tamure*, no? You come?'

She smiled at him. 'No,' she returned. 'My husband says we cannot come when you dance the *tamure*. Tell me about your boat.'

'Better I tell you about *tamure*,' the Polynesian laughed. 'Miri and me, we dance. Big night. Maybe you don't have breakfast tomorrow. No cook.'

And how in the world do I get the conversation back where I want it? Ask? Come right out with it? 'That's a long trip to Maupiti,' she said. 'What boat do you use?'

'Long trip? You go top of mountains, you can see Maupiti. Nine kilometres, maybe ten. This village has one *pahi*, one ocean-going canoe.' He gestured down the beach to the old pier. 'Easy trip. Good wind, quarter of one day. Bad wind, we paddle. Half a day. No problems. One day we go, you come with us?'

And that does it, Rose told herself exultantly. All I have to do is come down some Friday morning, get aboard, and away we go. Yes, sure, her mind nagged at her. And right at lunch time Giles finds I'm gone, he gets on the radio, and the police know all about it. Damn! It's an answer, but not the *right* one. I don't have enough information. How do I get information? Newspapers!

'Sam,' she called, as if it were an afterthought. 'Can you bring me back some newspapers the next time you go?' Apuka looked at her strangely.

'Bring back newspapers every trip,' he said cautiously. 'He don't let you read? Bring back Tahiti newspaper, New York paper, Paris newspaper. Every trip.'

'*Aue*,' she sighed. It seemed to be the only word that fit the occasion. 'He doesn't tell me. That man!'

The Polynesian grinned at her, flashing his beautiful white teeth. 'Best way to treat *vahine*,' he laughed. He picked up his wooden hammer, his length of sennet cord, and went back to work.

She went back up the beach whistling. So! Somewhere in that house are stacks of newspapers. And if Inspector Tihoni is right, her father's case would certainly be in the headlines. 'I've got you, Giles Gendron,' she whispered melodramatically. And then, more honestly. 'Well, I might only have a hold on your little toe.' And then after a few more steps. 'They're all chauvinists—every darn man on this island!'

Josie came running up at her first call. The little girl seemed subdued. They walked around the bay, waded the sparkling little river, and then started for the stairs that led up to the big house. The girl took Rose's hand with both of her own and tugged them to a stop.

'Mama?'

'Yes dear?' She leaned against the rickety rail that lined the steps. The child was bothered by something, and *that* should be ironed out immediately.

'Terri broke his finger.'

'He did? How did he do that?'

'It was something he was doing in his boat. But his mother said . . .' A pause, while the child fumbled with her words.

'What did his mother say?'

'His mother said there are many accidents in the village this month, and it's all your fault. That's what she said.'

Rose stared down at the girl. Those huge eyes in that small face were immense, and worry-lines chased across her little forehead. 'My fault? I don't understand.'

'They said it was bad luck, because you brought Pele down out of her mountain, and nobody would have no good luck until somebody carried her back up to her— to her something. I missed the word.'

'To her *maere*. Her little temple. You don't believe all that, do you?'

'I don't know, Mama. But that's what they said. They wasn't angry or nothing, just sort of sad. You know?'

'It's all superstition, love. That's all. Just superstition. Do you think the *tahu'a* would talk to us the way he did today if he thought we had desecrated Pele's temple?'

'Desa who?'

'Desecrated. Did bad things to it.'

'Oh I don't know Mama. All I know is what they said. That nobody on the island could have good luck until Pele goes home.'

'You *must* see that it's all nonsense,' Rose insisted. 'Why, Pele's just a little *tiki*, a little statue. It isn't really worth anything, and there's no way it could bring luck, good or bad. I'll get Mr Apuka to talk to them. Come on now, we're going to be late for supper!'

She put one arm around the girl and started up the stairs. But as they climbed another thought started to whip around in her head. If Pele is all that unimportant, she asked herself, how come you hang on to it with might and main. How come you just don't pack her up her mountain and set her back up in her little temple? How come? But like all her other little troubles, she could find no answer for this one either.

Giles watched them as they climbed up the stairs. Standing at the front of the veranda he could see how close they were. How little giggles of laughter started up in one, and spread to the other. How they looked at each other. He nursed his drink angrily. What the hell is wrong with me! I had a lucky escape when she turned down my marriage proposal. Wasn't one mistake enough? All these years, and I've still got Helen hanging around my neck like an albatross. He tapped the envelope in his pocket, just to be sure it was still there.

'Daddy!' The girl hurled herself across the intervening space and was swept up in his arms.

'Hey,' he protested. 'Cut out the wiggling. We saw each other at breakfast, you know.'

'I know,' Josie teased. 'You didn't shave.'

'Did I forget again? Did I scratch you?'

'No, you didn't scratch me, but you gotta be careful with Mommy. Her skin is more tenderer than mine.'

'More tenderer? Where in the world did you learn that?'

'I dunno. I been studying hard. Mommy's got soft skin, but a hard heart. She stands over me with a stick and makes me study!'

'I do no such a thing, young lady,' Rose objected.

'Well no,' the girl confessed. 'It was the *tahu'a* that had the stick!'

'You mean to tell me the *tahu'a* has been teaching you?'

'I'll tell you, but first you gotta kiss Mommy.' The

girl wiggled out of his arms and took Rose's hand. 'Well?'

'Well indeed.' He looked over the little girl's head at Rose's perfectly formed face. It was easy to read the succession of expressions that flashed across it. First, shock, then—fear? And then disdain, which gradually changed as she looked down at the girl between them. And then the look was—fatalistic?'

'Our daughter demands a free show,' he chuckled, holding out both hands. Rose hesitated for a second, pried her hand free from Josie's grip, and offered both to him. He stood in place until Josie gave Rose a push. She came into his arms reluctantly, but she did come. 'Smile,' he whispered in her ear as he pulled her close.

'I'd rather bite you,' she hissed back, baring her teeth. Before she could recover her stance his lips came down on hers, teasing, questing. He could see the muscles in her shoulders stiffen as she prepared to suffer but not give in.

'Remember the child,' he chortled softly as he came back to the assault. She stood her ground until his hand wandered down her back and gently caressed the soft swelling of her hip. He could feel the jolt that struck her. She actually jumped an inch, and then all her resisting muscles collapsed. Instantly he pressed closer. She sighed and gave herself up to the rising excitement. He broke off the contact, upset at her reaction as well as his own.

My God, he told himself, has it ever been like this with any other woman? Look at her standing there, trembling. She felt it, but she didn't want to. There's a tear in her eye. What do I do now? Here's one of the world's most desirable women, I can turn her on whenever I want to, but she hates it!

He dropped his hands away from her shoulders. 'Sorry,' he mouthed. She blinked at the tears, and wiped them away with a knuckle.

'What's the matter?' The girl tugged at Rose's skirt for attention. 'You got Daddy in your eye again?'

'I—I guess I have,' she murmured. And then in a stronger voice, 'Run along now, dear. Bathroom. And scrub those hands. Hurry up.'

After his daughter disappeared down the hall he waited for her anger. It didn't come. She stood in front of him, back straight, heels together, head down, hands clasped behind her back. And said nothing. He fumbled for a conversational *entrée*.

'You're not wearing your new dresses?'

'No,' she sighed.

More silence. 'We have a surprise for you for supper, Rose. Tonight we eat beef, courtesy of Dupont y Freres.'

The name re-awakened her memories. Letters. She smiled down at Josie, who came up and presented her little hands for inspection before sitting down.

'Oooh. Steak.' Josie's eyes sparkled as she snatched up the seldom used knife and fork by her plate. 'We ain't had no steak for three months.'

'We haven't had any,' Rose automatically corrected.

'Yeah.' The child managed to squirt the words out of a stuffed mouth. Letters, Rose reminded herself. Newspapers.

'We have a small problem in the schoolroom,' she began. He put down his fork and looked at her.

'We are supposed to be conducting a class in current events,' she continued doggedly. 'We need some newspapers.'

'Ah!' He went back to masticating his steak. She waited. Miri appeared with the dessert, a fruit and cheese tray. Josie was keeping both ears perked to the conversation. Next time, she promised herself. You won't get away with this forever, Mr High and Mighty!

He went back to his workroom after supper. She

could hear him slaving away at his machine as she walked down the hall after sorting the laundry and folding it away. Josie had dropped off to sleep immediately, so she went back out on the porch.

Tired herself, she relaxed in the lounge, half asleep. A shadow darker than the night impinged on her consciousness. Giles was there, squeezing his bulk into the lounge beside her. 'Miri's watching from the corner,' he announced, and leaned over to kiss her gently. 'Hold my hand. Polynesians have a lot of faith in hand-holding, but not in kissing.'

Dazed, she put her tiny hand in his and they sat quietly side by side for about ten minutes. She stirred, tugging at her hand. 'I think we can stop now,' she announced. 'I'm sure Miri must have gone home by now.'

'What?' It seemed as if he were coming out of a daydream. 'Miri? She went home right after supper.'

She could feel the rage mounting. One fierce shake recovered her hand. 'Damn you,' she hissed. 'Damn you!'

'Don't sizzle,' he chuckled. 'What's one little kiss?'

'With you there's no such thing as little,' she snarled at him. She used one hand to scrub her lips clean. 'I've told you before—don't you ever touch me again!'

'Okay, okay,' he sighed. The silence hung about them for another five minutes. 'I've a letter from my wife— from my former wife,' he announced. She looked over at him. He was thumbing an envelope. In the early moonlight he had a silvery look about him. All the heavy lines in his face were disguised. Why, he looks almost handsome, she told herself.

'I guess you know that it's her alimony that keeps us broke,' he mused. 'The judge in New York figured she needed five thousand a month to live on, and another two thousand a month to keep Josie.'

She could feel a certain amount of sympathy for him,

but refused to make it public. He watched her hair blowing in the breeze, and then continued. 'That's the way the ball bounces.' It was meant to be lightly said, but she could hear the bitterness in his voice. 'The American court system has this thing about mothers and children. They don't seem to care how bad the home is, or how little attention the child gets. Custody goes almost automatically to the mother. And the father pays. No wonder there's such an epidemic of kidnapping—fathers looking for their right to be a parent, even though it breaks the law.'

'Is that what you did? Kidnapped Josie?'

'Yes. I had to do something. I picked her up at her school, went back and beat the hell out of that guy Helen was living with, and hopped a plane.'

'And that brought you to Te Tuahine?'

'Eventually. Three years ago. Helen's been looking for us ever since. Using my money, of course. This letter was quite a surprise.'

'How so?'

'She wants to marry the guy.'

'Nothing wrong in that, is there?'

'No, that's good fortune. If she marries him, the alimony stops. But she's too clever to cut off her income. She writes to tell me she's *thinking* of getting married, and if I were to offer her an appropriate wedding present, she just might do that.'

'Appropriate?'

'Money. She's looking for a lump-sum settlement and she'll let me off the hook. Only I don't have the money. If the Indians were selling Manhattan Island again, I couldn't afford to buy Battery Park.'

'Oh!' She could feel his discouragement. Silence again. 'But you expect to make a great deal of money from this book?'

'Hey, after all the help you gave me, it's a sure winner. But that's future income.'

'Is your—is Helen a gambler?'

'How in the world did you know that? That's where all the money goes. Into the Atlantic City casinos. If I could burn down the Boardwalk at Atlantic City I could save a bundle.'

'Then I think there's a possibilty, Giles.'

'There is? Did you know that's the first time you called my by my given name in some time?' The darkness hid her blushes. She huddled away from him, into the farthest corner of her lounge.

'I was only kidding,' he said. 'What's your big idea?'

'Why don't you offer her a gamble. Offer her a quarter or a half—or all of the rights from this book. Everything. Movies, royalties, spin-offs. All in exchange for your freedom now.'

'Good lord,' he said, surprised. 'That could run into a half a million dollars if handled right. Maybe she *would* go for that sort of a bet.' He thought for a moment, and then stirred. 'I think I'll write her immediately.'

He leaned over in her direction as if to kiss her again. She squeaked a denial and slid off the edge of her chair. She could see him shake his head as he held himself stiffly poised, and then relaxed into the chair again. They both stared out over the water towards the village, where the faint sound of music was swelling up. Figures could be seen moving in the shadows of a bonfire.

'From the sound of the beat they're dancing the *tamure* tonight,' he chuckled.

'Yes,' she agreed softly.

'There's going to be more than one baby made tonight.' She let the comment pass. The compelling beat of the drums, the sweet sound of the guitars, the sparkling heavens of night, all were conspiring to mesmerise her. If only it could be different, she told herself. If only we didn't have all this anger and deceit between us.

'Do you still hate me?' His words dropped through her jumbled thoughts and reverberated around inside her head. Do I still hate him? It was a strain now for her to recall that night. All the passions, all the pain. Do I hate him? Or do I hate myself?

'Yes,' she managed to squeeze out, knowing it was a lie. She could hear his hissing sigh. He shifted noisily and got up. For a moment she thought he was going to come over to her, but instead he moved towards the door of the house. '*Iorana oe*,' he said softly, and went inside.

'Live happily ever after?' She sighed softly as his back disappeared. And the tears came, like a gentle spring rain.

CHAPTER NINE

IT was pleasant sitting in the sand by the grove of Royal palms. The bay shimmered in front of her, caught at that moment of change when the incoming tide just equalled the outpourings of the little river. A couple of elders from the village waited at the end of the rickety old pier. Out beyond the reef she could see the *pahi*, the ocean-going catamaran. It was pointed up into the wind, its huge sail fluttering, as the helmsman waited for just the right moment to run the passage in the coral barrier. It would be a while, she knew from experience.

For almost ten weeks now she had made it a weekly practice to meet the boat, collect the mail, and look at the newspapers. Ever since the evening when they had argued, Josie had cried, and he had stomped off, to return moments later and fling a newspaper in her lap. She had struggled with her dictionary. Spoken French she could handle. The printed word was something else. But the search of the thin Papeete paper was fruitless. There was no mention of Jules Lambert, or his daughter Rose Harriet. No mention that is, except for the two big holes cut in the front page. Something had been taken out. Something almost two columns wide. When she threw the paper to the floor in disgust he had glared at her and given her that steely laugh that seemed to be his favourite these days. And so, to avoid more censorship, she had begun to meet the mail boat, scanning the papers before he got his hands on them. Sam Apuka had no objections. 'Big House is not my affair,' he offered. 'Make you feel good to help your man, okay by me.'

148

Out in the ocean, perhaps a quarter of a mile behind the canoe, she could see the rain squall. Totally defined in that vast ocean space, it raced towards the island, dropping its rain in a huge circle. The sun shone around and through it, creating myriad rainbows. The watchers aboard the *pahi* saw it too. The paddles came out on the starboard side, gently swinging the double bows around, holding everything steady. And then, just at the right moment, the helm came down, the two sixty foot hulls swung over, and the squall filled the sail. The *pahi* changed from a listless log lying quiescent on the surface, to a charging living thing, racing for the channel with a froth at its bows.

'They lose the wind inside the lagoon,' the voice said behind her. The *tahu'a* dropped to the sand beside her. 'Takes twenty, thirty minutes to paddle. I have something to tell.'

She gauged the distance and admitted he was right. The sail bellied and flapped, and six paddles bit the water, there on each side. 'Something to tell me?' I might as well humour the old man, she thought to herself. He really is a nice fellow, in spite of all this mumbo-jumbo with mad goddesses and looks into the future. She gave him her best smile.

'So,' he sighed, adjusting his position. 'Pretty soon is high summer. The longest day of the year, just before Christmas.'

Although she knew it was true, she just hadn't thought about it. Christmas in the middle of summer? Her Louisiana blood objected! 'Yes,' she said. 'I had forgotten. I don't know what we can do to celebrate Christmas here.'

'You should not worry,' the old man assured her. 'You be gone by then.'

'Gone?'

'Gone from the island, *tamahine*.'

'I don't understand.'

'No, of course you don't. There is much pain coming to you, but by Christmas you be gone from island, and rainbow will shine for you. Providing you do a favour—a little favour—for Pele.'

Oh no, not that again, she thought. He can't really believe in all this nonsense. She made a quick check on the canoe as it glided through the green water of the lagoon. Still fifteen minutes, no less. Oh well. 'What sort of favour does Pele want?'

As usual, he approached the subject circuitously. 'Pele, goddess of volcanoes,' he began, 'and Tangora, god of seas. Since creation they fight each other. Pele shakes the earth, Tangora waits. See over there, the black sand? From long ago, when Pele shakes the mountain and it erupts. Lava burns everything it touches, but in the end it runs into the sea, and Tangora puts out fires.'

'So Pele is the *bad guy* and Tangora is the *good guy*?'

'No,' he laughed. 'You get it wrong. There is no good, no bad. Pele is woman, Tangora is man. Woman rages and shakes world, but only to limit man sets.'

'Oh wow,' she giggled. 'What a blow that is for woman's liberation!'

He smiled at her. 'Not to laugh,' he chided, but there was a twinkle in his eye. 'Pele and Tangora, since world begins, no? But now look. Pele sees over all the islands. The ways of the *popa'e* rule. New strong God in heaven. So Pele sends message. Take me to the new land, she says. I will shake the mountains for a new young people. Take me!'

'Good Lord. You want me to—Pele wants me to take her to the States? I—wow. And then what?'

'And that is all,' the old man said. 'Pele will do the rest.'

'But I can't do that,' she stammered. 'She's a *tiki*, an artifact. There's a law about exporting artifacts.'

'Not to worry,' the old man sighed. 'There are friends

and helpers. A case will be provided. No questions will be asked. You will?'

'Why, I——' She stopped to consider. Why not? At the very least the *tiki* would remind her of her strange stay on the island. Why not? 'Yes,' she nodded. 'If I can get her through customs, I'll take her.'

'Good. *Iorana oe, Tamahine.* The canoe is landing.'

She passed him a smile again, got up and sauntered down to the pier. She was familiar with the crew, but there was still that little wall between herself and the villagers, that distance dictated by the stories circulating. About Pele and herself, of course. They waved, they spoke, but never came close. So when Sam Apuka vaulted ashore he was as welcome to her as anyone could be. He slung the mail sack down and emptied it. The crew was unloading stores.

'Here. Four letters for the Big House.' Sam was sifting through the little pile. 'One for the *tahu'a*. Hey! And one for me!' He handed over the envelopes to her, along with the three regular papers.

'One for you, Sam?' she teased. 'The girl you left behind?'

'*Aue*,' he laughed. 'It comes from the CEP. I bet they want I come back to work for them, hey?'

'Would you, Sam?'

He waved a hand around him. 'Go back when I have all this? And my *vahine* too? Hah!'

'Well thank God for that.' She thanked him and started back down the pier, scanning the letters as she went. All for Giles, of course. Two from New York. She recognised Helen Gendron's scribbles. The other from his publisher. One letter from Portland Oregon. I don't even know where that is, she mused. And one from San Francisco, from his agent. She tapped all four letters against her palm as she manoeuvered around a particularly decayed section of the pier.

Strange how much I know about him, and how little.

We hardly ever speak, and yet—the nightly ritual on the veranda goes on. For Josie's sake, of course. One kiss, and one bout of hand-holding where the little girl can see it Nothing more. He talks more often about his book. Silly He rambles on and on about a problem, solves it himself and then gives me all the credit. I should have a hard job like that for the rest of my life! But the book is finished Now maybe he can relax. He works too hard.

Back among the palm trees she looked up, and ther made herself a little nest in the sand. You always look Sitting under a Royal palm is reasonably safe; sitting under a coconut palm is suicide! She set the letters aside and unrolled the week's issues of the Papeete paper Her French had improved considerably since she started her search. She thumbed her way through the first two days' issues and found nothing. In the third she had a nibble.

Banque Pacifique Tahiti Reopens in Temporary Quarters, the headline said. Laboriously scanning word for word she followed the one paragraph story. It only added to her puzzle. The original bank building had burned down, a case of arson. A new and temporary structure was opening next door. A picture showed the dedication. And then, the story recalled, 'Police believe they have the location of the embezzler, who made off with two million francs in cash and bearer bonds. The Banque is now operating under new management.'

And I should think so, Rose giggled to herself. Oh Papa, you told me it was only fifty thousand. How could there be two million francs in that little case? She shook her head, and went on. The rest of the papers told her nothing. She studied the advertisements on the last page. Four more days until December. The paper was dated November 26th. She shrugged her shoulders The dresses were pretty, but beyond her ken. She struggled up, made a single bundle out of all the papers and started up the beach.

When the shock hit her it was so great that she paused in mid-stride, frozen. The world was shut out. The children playing nearby were silent, even though their lips were moving. Oh God, she half-sobbed. It can't be! It was only once! She forced her mind to function. I came ashore on September tenth. It was September seventeenth when the Inspector left. Nothing happened in September. I was excited, disturbed. October? Nothing happened in October. Could I still have been disturbed? And now it's—now it's November. And nothing has happened in November! Oh God, no! Not this way! Almost automatically her hand went down to the slight mound of her stomach. It can't be, she assured herself. I won't let it be! But deep in her heart she knew it was.

He was waiting for her when she came up on to the veranda. 'Hi, mail-girl,' he offered. He had her drink in his hands, and almost dropped it when she pushed the little pile of mail at him.

'You look tired,' he said. 'Have a hard day?'

'I—yes,' she stammered, fighting back the tears.

'Come on over here and relax.' His firm hand on her elbow guided her to the shade and the lounge chairs. She collapsed into one, shuddering.

'Hey, are you coming down with something?' His solicitude was too much. She averted her head and let the tears come. He watched for a minute, then joined her on the lounger, pulling her up against his chest. As usual, he was dressed only in a pair of ragged shorts. She had not noticed it before, but the fuzz of soft curly hair that stretched across his chest at the nipples, ran down like the letter T to his navel. She rubbed against it for comfort. He cuddled her. Her mind ran like a caged animal. As if I didn't have enough troubles, she screamed at herself. There's no place you can run to escape pregnancy. You take it with you whereever you go. And *he* did it. What kind of a fool am I to nestle up to the man who did this to me? She sat up abruptly and pulled herself away from him. He opened his arms immediately and let her go.

'So,' he said, 'after all this time, you still hate me?'

'It's not something you would forget too soon,' she answered bitterly. 'Not if you were a woman.'

He sighed, picked himself up, and went back to the other chair. She could hear the rattle of paper as he attended to the mail. She sat quietly, still shivering, looking out over the harbour. Josie came running out of the house.

'Mommy!' She ran across the veranda and threw herself at Rose. They tangled in a happy pile, hugging each other desperately. 'You been cryin' again,' the girl accused. 'Did Daddy get something in your eye again?' Josie looked across at her father accusingly.

He held up both hands in denial. 'Not me! I didn't have a thing to do with it.'

'You better not,' the child threatened, and turned back to nuzzle Rose's cheek. He went back to his letters again. The little girl chattered merrily away. 'Miri showed me how to make *poi,*' she laughed. 'It isn't as hard as you said, Mom. I got it right for the first time, and we're going to have it for supper. Wonderful?'

'Wonderful.' It was impossible to sit next to this little bundle of dynamite and not join in. 'All wonderful,' she chortled. 'How did I ever get such a smart daughter?'

'The stork brought me,' the girl giggled, 'Did you know that Miri is making a baby? She just told me about it. Her and Mr Apuka.'

'Oh Lord,' Rose exclaimed. 'I can see we have to speed up your biology course, love.'

'Did I say something wrong? Couldn't Miri do it all by herself?'

'No, baby, it takes two.'

The girl collapsed in Rose's arms again. He lifted his

head from his reading to watch them. That's right, she told herself. It takes two. I can't blame him for everything. Well, I can but I shouldn't. Look at the furrows on his face. They're deeper than ever before. He works too hard—and worries too much.

'I have a letter from your—from Helen,' he announced. Josie clung more tightly to Rose. 'She agrees to the proposal I made her. Would you believe that, she agrees!'

'What proposal was that,' Rose asked, her curiosity unlimited. Why is it that every time he mentions his— Helen, I get angry, she asked herself.

'I told her about the new book,' he reported, 'and offered her fifty per cent of all the royalties and movie rights. She write that she has been to Simpson & Savage, and she likes what they already have. And she talked to Morrie Burnbaum, my agent. He told her about the two movie offers he already has. And she agrees.'

'She agrees? What do *you* get?'

He smiled for the first time. 'I get to read her wedding announcement in the papers,' he chuckled. 'And she agrees to drop all prosecution concerning the —er—kidnapping.'

'And the alimony?'

'It ends the minute she says *I do*. But——'

'Of course. There's a "but".'

'Well, Helen was always a cautious gambler. She says that *her* lawyer has drawn up a contract, and Morrie has okayed it. But she's coming here before she signs. She has no intention of casting herself adrift until she's seen that the last chapters are finished.'

'She's very trusting, too, I gather.'

'Very. I don't know when she's coming. I can hardly read her hen-tracks.'

'I hope she never gets here,' Josie said sullenly. 'I hope her canoe leaks, and Pele gets her!'

'Josie!' Both adults spoke at the same time. The child sprang to her feet, staring at them with wide eyes.

'Well I do,' she shouted, and ran back into the house.

Supper that night was a silent affair. Josie refused to speak to either of them, even when Miri brought the *poi* to the table. Rose was quiet too, but for a different reason. Seeing Miri, so proud in her pregnancy, drove a sharp splinter into Rose's heart. All through the meal she sat on the edge of her chair, barely able to repress the shivering. He kept his eye on her, which only made things worse. It's not all his fault, her conscience yelled at her, but she refused to accept that judgment. It *had* to be his fault, she repeated. If I don't blame him, then I have to blame myself. And that would really crack me up. It's his fault!

And so to bed, where in the darkness, muffled by her own pillow, she could cry enough to ease the pain. The dreams came back. The taste of salt spray and death on her lips. The wild tossing of the little raft. The shivering cold of the tropical night. When sleep finally came it brought no rest with it.

Somewhere in the dark pre-dawn she felt a stirring at her bedside, and struggled to get one eye open. Josie was there, clutching her three-foot teddy-bear close against her chest.

Rose threw back to the corner of the sheet in invitation, and the child slid in beside her. 'What is it, love,' she asked softly pulling the small head into her bosom.

'When—when *she* comes, you won't let her take me. Please?'

'I—no, I won't let her take you.' I don't know how I'll keep that promise, but I won't let her take you, she promised again under her breath. I wish I knew an easy answer.

'And you'll be my Mama forever and ever?'

Rose hugged the little body tightly and sighed. 'Your Daddy has to decide that, baby. Now close your eyes and let's get some sleep. We have a great deal of studying to do tomorrow.'

'You mean *I* gotta,' the girl giggled, and promptly dozed off.

And now see what you've done, Rose lectured herself. It's not all that simple. Let him decide? Why did I say a stupid thing like that? I can't stay, not with——

Her hand slid down and rested on her stomach, and she dozed off herself.

It was a lethargic day that followed. Everyone in the house except Miri seemed to be infected with sleepy eyes. Rose struggled to keep Josie's nose in the books, but it was a losing battle. So when the flutter-sound came down the wind at eleven o'clock everyone on the island stopped to watch. As the noise grew louder even Giles broke away from his work and came out to watch.

'Helicopter,' he told them. 'That's an expensive way to travel around these parts. It must be flying in from Bora Bora.'

Very suddenly the Alhouette was upon them, coming in from the west over the twin peaks of the Sisters, hovering over the Big House, where there was hardly enough flat space to spin a top, and then coming to rest on the beach at the foot of the stairs. The motor noises dwindled, and only the whap-whap of the idle blades could be heard.

The overhang of the hill blocked off a good view of what was happening. The door of the helicopter opened and a woman climbed out, ducking her head under the threat of the big blades. A man in casual clothes—the pilot—climbed out of the other side of the machine and gestured towards the stairs. A second man, portly, white-haired, struggled out and looked around him. The pilot began to unload bags, stacking them in a pile on the sand. The other two started off towards the Big House.

'Ooh,' Josie said. She didn't sound happy at all.

'I can't believe it,' Giles muttered. 'It's Helen. A day after I got her letter, and here she is. Damn! Rose?'

He drew her aside, out of range of Josie's ears. 'I know it's an imposition,' he sighed, 'but I've got to ask. It will make things easier for Josie—and for me—if you would play my wife to the hilt while Helen is here. Please?'

She stared at him. The worry furrows were deeper than ever, but she was too sleepy to debate. 'All right,' she returned.

'Thanks,' he said laconically. 'It gives me another bargaining chip, if she thinks I've got a wife to take care of Josie.' His hand urged her back to the veranda, where the child was still waiting. Impatient, Rose rubbed her fingers along the plain gold ring she still wore on her right hand. Why am I concerned, she asked herself fiercely. It's only his former wife. Why should I care? There was no good answer, and the woman was coming up the steps.

'Giles!' The newcomer offered a cheek. He pecked at it. 'And Caroline!' She held out her arms to the girl, who promptly shrank away from her, dodging behind Rose's skirts.

'My name isn't Caroline,' the child muttered. 'Josie, that's my name. Josie.'

'No kiss for your mother?'

'You're not my mother. Rose is my mother!' The two skinny arms came around Rose's waist, where she clung like a limpet. And then, to be sure her point was taken, 'Rose is my mother.'

'Well really, Giles. I would have thought you would bring her up better-mannered than this.'

'I did,' Giles said. His voice was like steel. 'We did. Helen, this is my wife Rose.'

'This *is* a surprise!' Rose took a deep breath and stepped forward, offering a hand. It was ignored. 'I had not heard you were married, Giles. What a—curvaceous creature she is. You should diet, my dear. Slim is the word in the world of society this year.'

'She's just the way we like her,' Giles snapped. 'And in our society, she's perfect.'

'Welcome to Te Tuahine,' Rose murmured. One eyeful of this tall thin creature was enough. One earful was one too many. The woman was dressed in pure silk, a flaming scarlet. It seemed out of place with her dark eyes, her jet-black hair, her aura of sophistication.

'You almost make me believe that you are Caroline's mother,' Helen commented wryly. 'Look at you both. Blonde hair, green eyes, wide smile. Where in the world did you find this pixie, Giles?'

'Come into the house,' Giles snapped. 'You *are* here for business, aren't you?'

'Oh yes,' Helen responded. 'Nothing but. The sooner I can get this over with the better off I'll feel. The pilot said he had to go over to Maupiti to refuel. He'll come back for us tomorrow morning. That ought to be enough time to settle things, won't it?'

'Come alone, did you? Where's your lapdog?'

'You mean Jim, don't you. You'll never learn to take him seriously, will you. He's a fine artist, a great talent, just waiting to be discovered. He stayed behind in Tahiti. He felt nervous about coming to this primitive little island. And besides, the bank man who offered us a helicopter lift, said that another passenger would overcrowd things.'

'I'm glad he stayed in Tahiti,' Giles snorted. 'Every time I think about what he did to Josie I get the mad urge to punch him out again. Come inside. Rose, could you have one of the girls bring us some refreshments? Rose?'

They all turned to stare at her. She was standing at the edge of the porch, her mouth half open, one hand holding gently to the roof pillar. Her entire world was concentrated in what she saw. Everything else was shut out. The rotund figure of the man was just now puffing his way up over the top stairs. The man arrived. There was no better description of it. He put both his feet together on the top stair, brushed off his white suit, took off his white Panama hat, and mopped his brow. A squeal of recognition vibrated in Rose's throat, and suddenly she was down the stairs and running full speed towards him. He turned around just in time to catch her in his arms.

'Papa,' she screamed. 'Papa! I *knew* you weren't dead. I *knew* it!'

'Rose. Darling Rose!' They hugged each other in a frenzy of happiness, swaying back and forth and ignoring the trio on the porch. When they stopped to catch a breath he beamed down at her. 'And I knew you weren't dead, Rose. But that idiot, Inspector Tihoni, didn't tell me about you until the night before last. Unbelievable! Here I am the hero of Papeete, and he waited for three months to tell me.'

'Oh Papa, I don't care how long he waited. I just— how did you get to come in—the police? They haven't arrested you?'

'Later, my dear,' he whispered in her ear. 'Later. You wouldn't believe! I am the best friend the police force ever had. Can you imagine that policeman? *Did you know*, he said, *that there's a Rose Harriet Gendron out on Te Tuahine? A beautiful young lady, with a beautiful daughter!* Pah! And what scheming have you been up to Rosalie?'

'Later, Papa, later,' she whispered, mimicking him. 'Oh my dear, I'm so glad to see you. So glad. Even if they arrest us both!'

'Hush,' he cautioned. 'There will be no arresting, *chérie*.' She took his immaculate soft hand and pressed it against her cheek, then drew him back up to the veranda.

'Don't tell me,' Giles chuckled as he came down a couple of steps to meet them. 'Mr Lambert?'

'Just so. And you are?'

'I'm your son-in-law,' Giles announced. 'What a pleasant surprise. Do come into the house.'

'Mommy,' Josie chimed in. 'This is *your* daddy?'

'Yes love, this is my daddy.'

'Then he's my grandfather, isn't he?'

Her father seemed to stagger, Rose thought. She helped him to a chair on the veranda. 'You're not well, Papa?'

'Oh I'm very well indeed,' he laughed, wiping his forehead again. 'But as you can see, for a man of my age to meet my daughter's husband and find that I am already a grandfather, *ma foi*. It takes some doing, that?'

'Oh you fraud,' she laughed. The clear unfettered notes flew up to the housetop. She had not laughed like this since—since long before they had come to Tahiti. And her father! He would never grow old gracefully, but would have to be dragged, kicking and screaming, into old age. Always a man for the ladies. Always forgetting—purposefully, on which side of sixty he stood! 'Take off your jacket, Papa. Josie, help your grandfather with his coat, please.'

She was all smiles as she turned back to Giles and Helen. 'You go ahead, darling,' she said. Put in all the charm, she commanded herself. Here's my ticket out of this place. Keep him sweet until take-off time! 'I'll get one of the girls to bring you both something. In your study?' There now. That sounded so much better than 'workroom'. A little class, that's what I need to add. Papa always brings out the best in me!

'Yes, in the study.' There was laughter behind the solemn words. He knows exactly what I'm doing, she told herself, as the pair of them walked off. A well-matched pair. Both tall and slim, walking like a panther and his mate. They look so well together. So why does that give me a pain?

Josie was chattering away with her new grandfather when Rose came back from the kitchen. And somehow *that* gave her a little twinge too. He's *my* father, she told herself angrily. I don't want to share him with anybody! What am I saying. I'm jealous of the little girl? She handed her father the tall vodka and juice that he preferred, and sat down across the table from him.

'Josie,' she commanded. 'I need to be alone with my Papa. Go help Miri in the kitchen.'

'I wanna stay, Mama.' The child's face screwed up almost into tears. But Rose was so excited that she failed to notice. The little girl's shoulders drooped as she walked away.

'Now,' she said softly. 'They can't hear in the study. Listen.' Briefly but completely, she sketched out her life for the past months, leaving out only that—terrible night—and her pregnancy. 'I didn't know where you were, Papa. I thought anything I said or did might compromise you.'

'So.' He slipped at his drink. 'Then you are not married. That is too bad, *chérie*. He is your type of man.'

'Nonsense.' She brushed aside any idea of painting Giles in better colours. 'I hate the man. Now, quick, tell me about you!'

Her father stretched. 'This is lovely,' he reported. 'It was a long trip, that. Now, where to begin.'

'With the storm,' she coaxed. She tucked her legs up underneath her and gave him a happy smile.

'So.' He reflected for a moment. 'Well, Rose, sending you off in the life raft was a foolish thing to do. No sooner were you gone than the yacht broke loose from the rocks and then winds pushed us up into Apiri Cove and smashed us up on the beach as pretty as can be.

managed to get off, and wandered inland until I came to a village. Two days later the police came, and took me back to Tahiti. I thought our goose was cooked. Mind you, there I was carrying the brief case with all the money in it, and they came and carried me off.' He stopped and took another pull at his drink.

'But this, Rose, you'll never believe. The night that you and I—er—left Tahiti, somebody set fire to the bank building. That Emile Lorange, you remember him? The bank president? He set fire to the building to cover some of his- er—financial transactions, and then he left on the Qantas flight to Sidney. It's—er—hard to believe, Rose darling, but he embezzled two million francs in cash and securities!'

'Papa? You mean that? The same weekend? Two million?'

'All true, love. It made me feel—almost—inadequate!'

'And then what happened?'

'Well, the chief bookkeeper had been out yachting with his daughter when that terrible typhoon came up, right? They welcome me with open arms. I reconstruct the books from what was left—and from memory, and presto—I am a local hero. And now that the bank is open again, me—I am appointed by the board of directors to be the new president. What do you have to say about that, Rose Harriet!'

'Oh Papa!' She was laughing so hard that her stomach hurt, and that brought her back down to earth. 'Oh Papa,' she giggled, 'Uncle François always said it, didn't he.'

'Said what, love. Your uncle was always talking.'

'He said that you dip your hand into a bucket of grease and come out with a pearl! You are the president? They've hired the wolf to guard the sheep!'

'Now, now,' he said, doing his best to appear dignified. 'It is not that at all, Rose.'

'Then tell me what it is. Quickly, Papa. It's almost time for them to come out.'

'Ah, Rose. This is, perhaps, the hardest part to believe.' He stopped to clear his throat. 'I am now a man of the world, you recognise, *ma petite*. I aid the police to track down that—that dirty swindler. I am an authority at the bank. And very suddenly it all feels very good. Your Papa has decided to settle down, Rose Harriet. To be a man of honour and distinction.'

Rose looked at him suspiciously. 'Another scam, or another woman?' she asked.

'Ah, how sharp the arrows,' he sighed. 'I am a changed man, my Rosalie. As it happens, also, there is a woman. The little widow Marceau—you remember her?'

'You mean the widow with all that money, Papa?'

'The very same, my dear. As soon as I get back to Tahiti with my lovely daughter, the widow and I will make the marriage, no?'

Rose shook with gales of laughter. My father is a changed man? Horsefeathers. But she remembered the widow Marceau very well indeed. There would be an iron hand under that velvet glove. Whips would be cracked. Paths would become extremely straight and narrow. And there would be no place for a twenty year old pregnant daughter! Rose winced as that idea drifted across her mind. But there could be a lot of loving, and Papa needs that! She laughed until tears came to her eyes. And then they talked, covering the details left out the reminiscences recalled, until at last Miri rang the dinner gong, and they started for the dining room arm in arm. In the hall they passed Josie, standing with her back against the wall, crying. But Rose was too far gone in her own needs and loves to notice.

The meal was later than usual. But when Giles and his former wife came out of the study Helen was smiling broadly and clutching a multi-page legal document to her very slender frame. There was chatter around the table, but most of it went over Rose's head. She was deep in her daydreams, sitting beside her father, and reliving all the joys they had shared. Why, I believe I worship my father, she told herself happily. Josie was very quiet too. She crowded her chair in beside her adopted mother, bent her golden head over her plate, and toyed with her meal.

'And so you see,' Mr Lambert said expansively, coming to the end of one of his interminable stories, 'We go back to Tahiti together, my lovely Rose and I, for the marriage. Such a lucky girl, the widow Marceau!'

'Papa, don't be such a complete egotist,' she teased him. 'You may be God's gift to the female sex—and then again—well, you are getting a little long in the tooth, remember!'

Her father answered something. She had no idea what it was. Her eye had been caught by Giles in that second before her father answered. There was a look of—loss—that was the word. Sadness. He held her gaze, almost as if he were trying to hypnotise her. She struggled to break free, and succeeded only when Helen caught at his arm and broke his concentration.

The little girl tugged at Rose's sleeve. She bent her head over to hear better amid all the noise. 'You're really going away, Mommy?'

She heard the words, but not the import. She was far too busy making up for the missed months, learning to love her father all over again. 'Yes,' she answered quickly. 'With my father for his wedding day. It's a very special day.' The child said not another word for the rest of the night.

An hour later, acting her hostess role to the full, she parcelled them all out. 'Papa, you'll take the—er—spare room. Helen, you'll sleep in Josie's room. Josie, you'll share my room with me. Now——'

'And how about me?' Giles asked, with a sound of mock grievance in his voice. She gave him her brightest smile.

'We're cramped for space, sweetheart,' she pouted. 'So I thought—just this once—on the veranda? Those lounge chairs fold all the way back, and perhaps you wouldn't be *too* uncomfortable?'

CHAPTER TEN

It was an amalgam of many things that sent Rose into her first deep sleep in months. Meeting her father again, safe.The sleepless nights prior to this one. The excessive worry over her pregnancy. The wild wish that struck her at the dinner table, to know—to really know—what Giles thought and believed. Strange thought, that, considering how much she really hated him. But she fell asleep before Josie did, and awoke in the morning when the helicopter, coming back from its refuelling mission on Maupiti, buzzed the house and sent the teeming jungle birds into wild protests.

All the noise brought her up in her bed, startled. It took a moment for her to remember where and who she was. Amnesiac, she told herself, laughing. Josie was nowhere to be seen, and there was packing to do.

She jumped out of bed, wrapping herself carelessly in a pareau, and began to do just that. Someone had located an old battered suitcase for her. She stuffed it with her fanciest new underwear, added a few essential blouses and skirts, and snapped it shut.

I can get everything else—including a dress for the wedding—in Papeete, she told herself. And for travelling? Something cool but substantial. One of the sleeveless blouses she had made for herself, and a wraparound skirt to go with it. And rubber sandals. Lord, won't it be nice to buy a pair of real shoes. And to have a steaming hot bath, with lots of bubbles! A day or two of relaxation, and then I'll go to Papa's wedding, and then—she stopped herself there, determined not to think a single moment beyond the wedding.There was something that her subconscious knew that her conscious mind didn't want to hear. Just as far as the wedding, that's the ticket. She slipped her feet into the thong of the rubber sandals and made for the door.

The others were already on the veranda. All except Giles.

'Ah, at last,' her father pontificated. 'I thought we would have to go without my Rose!' He offered her a big hug, and kissed the tip of her nose.

'Yes, do please hurry,' Helen said. 'I need to get out of this primitive backwater as soon as possible. Back to civilization and the bright lights, that's for me.' The woman's hand patted the briefcase under her arm as if it contained the crown jewels. And maybe it does, Rose thought. How in the world did Giles ever get caught up with her? Cold—even in the tropical heat of December. Every one of her words drips ice.

'The pilot is waving.' Her father interrupted her thoughts. 'We will go now, *chérie*.' He took her arm in a proprietorial way, and ushered her down off the veranda, just as Giles laboured up the steps in front of them, two at a time.

'Rose,' he called. 'Have you seen Josie? We can't find her.'

A chill struck at Rose's heart. Josie! In one overwhelming flash she recalled all the separate little scenes from the day before. All the times she had brushed the child aside. All the self-centred neglect. 'I—I haven't seen her,' she returned anxiously. 'She—I—I fell asleep very quickly last night. I thought she was—Miri?' The Polynesian girl had come up to them.

'No. Not in the village,' Miri reported. 'I don't see her at sunrise, when I come to make *le petit dejeuner*. Nobody sees her. Sam say he will send out searchers at once, no?'

'We can't wait for some silly child,' Helen snapped. 'Come on, Mr Lambert, let's go.'

Rose's hand itched, wanting badly to slap her face.

'Even if it's *your* silly child that's missing?' She made fists, tight tiny balls, looking for someone to pound.

'Ah, it is a small thing,' her father soothed. 'The island is small. There is no way to get off. Come on Rose, we go now.'

'Really,' Helen remarked in a slow drawl. 'I can hardly spare another minute in this—this island paradise.'

'No,' Rose said stubbornly. 'I can't go until I'm sure Josie is safe!' There was more than stubbornness there. All this time I've been blaming him for everything, she told herself grimly, and I didn't pay a bit of attention to my *own* responsibilities. The poor little kid! I knew she wanted me as a surrogate mother, and I just brushed her off. All because I was so wrapped up in my own concerns. Be honest with yourself at least, Rose. All because you wanted to retreat to your own childhood—to be safe and cosseted by your father—to go back to when life was simpler! Damn! The guilt feeling was too much for her to bear alone. She moved closer to Giles, pleading silently for his support. Without even looking, one of his hands dropped down on her shoulder and gently squeezed.

'I'm not going,' she confirmed. 'You go ahead, Papa. When I can, I'll come. After we find Josie.'

'You're sure, child?'

'It's something important, Papa. I *have* to do it. It's my fault. I'll come when I can.'

'Well——' Her father fussed with the idea, but a look at her determined chin convinced him. 'Of course, Roasalie. You'll come when you can.' He turned to Giles. 'And you, Mr Gendron. You will have good luck in finding your daughter, and you will take care—special care—of mine, no?'

'Yes.' Giles smiled for the first time that day. Her father cleared his throat, shrugged his shoulders, and started off. Why he's getting more Gallic every day,

Rose thought as she watched him disappear down the stairs to the beach.

Rose gave a weak half-wave, and wondered what was happening to her. At any other time, any other place, she would have followed her father off to whatever adventure awaited. But not now. Her feet seemed glued in place, and her conscience thumped on her with a myriad of guilty feelings. *If only I had,* she told herself, recounting the litany of things she *should* have done to reassure the child. *But then, I never really thought it out. All the time I was accepting the child's love—yes, and giving in return—I never thought what would happen when it was time to go!* 'There's another mess you've gotten us into,' she muttered in her favourite Laurel and Hardy imitation. It brought a weak smile to her face, but no more. Giles was coming back out of the house. She turned to him as naturally as if he were a friend, rather than the man she hated.

'What can I do?' she asked.

'Do? Why—it's no use your running up and down, Rose. We've got plenty of people for that. You can do the most good just by staying here and keeping track of where everyone else is. And, who knows, Josie might come wandering back at any minute. Why the devil are you crying now? You could have gone with your father. Maybe it's not too late?'

She put a hand on his arm. 'I'm crying about Josie,' she sniffed. 'I don't *want* to go with my father. If I had been a little wiser, Josie would still be here!' She was interrupted by a swell of sound from the beach. The helicopter pulled itself up, dipped a salute over the roof of the Big House, and headed westward for the gap between the Sisters.

'Here now,' he offered, wrapping her up in a comforting arm. 'It wasn't your responsibility. She's my daughter. I've been too damn distracted by all the fancy manoeuvring going on. I'm the one to blame. Now, I've got to get wheeling. You stay here, right?'

'Right.' Her answer was a soft murmur, but he caught it and returned a warm smile before he plunged down the path on the other side of the house. 'Where are you going now?' she called after him.

He stopped and shook his head. 'We have to cover all the bases,' he called back throatily. 'A couple of the men are dragging the pond behind the dam.'

'Oh God!' She stuffed her fist to her mouth. Dragging the pond! The girl wanted a mother. And what a terrible mother I've made for her! She found her way blindly back to the kitchen, where Moera was busy at the cooker.

'Men get hungry,' the young Polynesian girl offered.

'Yes,' Rose returned, and pitched in to help.

She worked hard until noon, and then went out on the porch as the workers came in to report, snatch at the lunch, and head back out again. Giles did not show up. After the clean-up in the kitchen, Rose stumbled back out on to the veranda and collapsed into a lounge chair. It was the first free minute since the helicopter had taken off. The first time to really think about her problem. And with nobody within a mile of the house, she brooded.

The child needs me. For some stupid reason she seems to think that I'm a nice person. Which I certainly am not. And that's not the whole of it. I need Josie as much as she needs me! And *there* was a revelation that startled her. I need Josie? Of course I do. I love that child as if she were my own. And how is that possible? She's the daughter of the man I hate. Well, perhaps hate is too strong a word. But at least I dislike him. And that's too weak a word. So I hate him. And why not, after all he's done to me!

Her hand wandered down unconsciously and stroked her stomach. God, what do I do now? I've got to leave this crazy place. I've got to get away from this man. But I can't really escape him, can I? I'll be carrying him with me, whereever I go. His son will look like him, and I'll be haunted for the rest—now why did I say his *son*? Maybe it will be his daughter! Another conversation flashed across her mind. She had been talking to Miri about the baby the Polynesian girl was expecting. 'And is not a boy,' Miri had laughed, 'I have to try again, no?'

Rose stifled the little sob that caught in her throat. In the end I have to leave. And that means Josie will have to stay behind. And there we'll be—me, his son, and Pele—wandering the earth like Judas? Condemned to haunt the world forever? She leaned back in her chair, and, unprepared for the attack, fell into the arms of sleep.

Giles came back to the house at five o'clock, worn to the bone. She was still asleep, sprawled over the lounger in wild sexy disarray. For a second he thought of waking her, of touching that soft creamy skin, of crushing her up against him—but he fought off the urge, the mad desire. He went into the house, showered, changed into a dry pair of shorts, and went out again. There were shouts, and a conch-shell sounded from the shoulder of Mona Aui. He shrugged his shoulders into a dry T-shirt and started off in that direction.

She woke up just as the sun tipped the top of the Sisters, spraying a rainbow of colour across the bottom side of the few fluff clouds which were hurrying southward. A pale pink glow illuminated the permanent cloud that stood over Pele's mountain. The cloud associated the name. Immediately she thought of the little *tiki* standing in her bedroom. Pele. And it awakened a suspicion.

She threw off the light cover that someone had draped over her legs and sprinted to the bedroom. In the half-light of dusk there were too many shadows. She pumped up the Coleman lantern and lit it. The white, almost fluorescent light, dispelled the gloom. A quick look told her all she needed to know. The *tiki* was gone. And what had Josie said? 'They all think you brought bad luck when you brought Pele down the mountain. You hafta take her back!' Yes of course, Rose thought. 'You hafta take her back.' Josie has gone up Pele's mountain to take the *tiki* back!

There was nobody else in the house. She snatched the lantern, a packet of matches, and threw the remainder of a cold supper into a pandanus-woven basket. Giving no thought to notes for others, she grabbed up the basket, raced out the door, and dived into the jungle growth behind the house.

It was as much a struggle as it had been that first time. The paths were still overgrown, and with the onset of darkness the way became even more difficult. She held the lantern up in front of her and struggled upward, paying no attention to the barbs and briars that tore at her clothes and scratched her legs and arms. Occasionally there was a noise in the undergrowth that startled her. Frightened her half out of her wits, if the truth be told. But she kept going. It was fully dark when she stumbled into the clearing half way to the top of the mountain. Fully dark, and no moon. She made her way cautiously over to the rock outcropping, and crumpled up in a little heap, panting for breath. Her shoulder was sore where she had carelessly bounced off a breadfruit tree. Down below her she could see the lights of the village and the Big House. There were no lights on the other mountains. Evidently the search had been called off. 'Oh Josie,' she moaned. 'You have to be here. You have to!' And then swore aloud, in the heat of her grief, 'I'll never leave you again, Josie. Never!'

It seemed right to say it, even though the saying raised a host of spectres behind it. You can't have Josie without Giles, she told herself, and laughed hysterically. What in the world would I want Giles for! If there is ever a man who—and suddenly even the artifice of her fake marriage was too much for her. She struggled with the ring that he had placed on her left hand, tore it off, and threw the offending circlet over the edge of the cliff. And then it was time to go. She picked up the basket in one hand, the lantern in the other, and plunged back into the dense growth above her.

Giles came back to the house just after sunset. He could not disagree with the elders. There was nothing to be gained by further searching in the night. The house was dark as he stumbled up the stairs on to the veranda. 'Rose?' The house echoed silence. He went in, stomping down the hall to her room. His legs were tired, worn beyond belief. 'Rose?' He flexed his muscles, trying to readjust them. He muttered to himself as he wandered back to the dining room, and then out to the kitchen. The lamp smoked for a second, and then settled down. There was nothing to be seen. Nothing except the scattered remains of the supper. He snatched at a cold piece of rib, pulled a can of beer out of the cooler, and went back out on to the porch.

A cooling wind fanned his face as he leaned against the doorpost and scanned the world spread out in front of him. A few fires flickered in the village. Everything looked peaceful. What a deception, he told himself. Somewhere in all this blackness is my daughter! And if I had the sense God gives little children, I would have paid some attention to her instead of that stupid mother of hers. But I was too busy buying Helen off to notice. Where the hell is Rose?

He had gnawed the bone clean. Disgusted with life, he hurled it out on to the hillside. It would be picked dry by morning. The tropical night was like that. Where the hell is Rose! The poor woman was—yes, almost as badly off as Josie must be—when I left her. Tired, dispirited, blaming herself for things that were not her fault! You're a fool, Gendron, to think you could blackmail her into being Josie's mother. An arrogant

stupid fool. And if you hadn't seduced the poor kid—
well, who knows what might have happened. Luckily
she didn't get pregnant!

He shook himself, like a dog coming out of the water.
Lucky? I've been nothing but bad luck to that poor
kid—to that poor sexy woman! Nothing but bad luck!
Somewhere in the back of his mind there was an itch he
could not scratch. He finished off the beer, crushed the
can, and set it down on the veranda table.

The bending over brought his eye level down far
enough so he could see up the mountain. Up the
mountain of Pele, where a single bright light glowered
at him, blinked, and was gone.

'My God,' he shouted to the world. 'That crazy kid!
Rose!' He roared it twice, and then twice again. The
light was gone. He ran for the kitchen, for the spare
Coleman lantern, the medical kit, and the emergency
food kit. 'Think!' he yelled at himself. But the
impatience—the driving mind-boggling impatience, was
too much. Taking what he had already assembled, he
ran for the mountain path.

It was almost midnight when Rose stumbled wearily
to the lip of the crater. And still no moon. There was a
dull outline of clouds in the distant east, and some of
the familiar stars were blotted out. The sweet scents of
jasmine, vanilla, gardenias, flooded her senses. She
stood at the broken edge of the chasm and took deep
breaths, pumping new life into her body. A slight breeze
kissed her scratched and bleeding cheek. She pumped
up the lantern again, and started down into the crater.

It was more difficult than the first time. Then she
had both hands free, the moon was up, and she was
not so driven by fear. Now all she could think of was
the child. A mad litany repeated itself over and over
again, so much so that she was not sure she was
thinking or talking. 'Josie! Josie! Josie!' Just the name,
nothing more. But if she were speaking, the name

contained all the love, all the fears, that knit her to the little girl.

She was lucky, at that. The lantern both helped and blinded her, and she almost stepped into the lake before her tired senses told her she had reached her destination. She stopped and held the lantern high.

'Josie,' she yelled at the top of her voice. 'Josie!'

'Mama?' The voice was weak, filled with disbelief. 'You didn't go? Did you come for me?'

The sound came from her left, deep in the underhang of the cliff where Pele's *maere* stood. There was no more time for thought. She dropped the basket and ran. The darkness seemed to be filled with haunting dangers, but it parted in front of her, pushed aside by lantern light. And there, at the foot of the *maere*, was a crouching little body.

Don't get her excited, Rose told herself. Be calm. Don't let her know that you're frightened half to death! You're the adult. You're ten years older than she is. Get a grip on yourself. You're her mother!

The lecture helped. She set the lantern down on the smooth top of the *maere*, and dropped down beside the little girl. 'Josie love,' she coaxed softly, and opened her arms. A warm soft body crowded in on her, and a trembling voice wailed, 'Mommy, Mommy,' as the girl squirrelled against her, trying to bury herself in the softness. Rose squeezed hard. It comforted the child, and it helped *her* to control her shaking muscles.

'It's all right, baby,' she soothed. 'Mommy's here. Did you bring Pele back home?'

'Yes. She's up there.' The girl pointed. Rose stretched, just enough to bring her head to the level of the *maere*. Pele squatted there, teetering on the edge, shadowed by the bright light of the lantern. Oh brother, Rose sighed to herself. At this rate they'll have me believing in little volcano goddesses too! Keep your cool. Don't let the child know how frightened you are.

She dropped back to her knees beside Josie. Her searching hands found no broken bones, no cuts, no blood. 'You're not hurt, baby?'

'No, but it got dark, and I was scared to go back down. You didn't go in the helicopter?'

'Yes, I went,' she chuckled. That's it, her brain commented. Get a little humour in the situation, Rose. 'Yes, I went with my father,' she repeated. 'I'm not really here, you know!'

She felt a sharp pinch on her bottom. 'Hey, ouch,' she complained.

'You are too here,' the little girl laughed. 'You are too. I was cold, and you're so warm!' The child's head dived into Rose's breasts, seeking that warmth. Rose squeezed again. The tears stopped.

'I brought us some food,' Rose thought to say. 'Wait here a minute while I——'

'No, Mommy. If you're going someplace, so am I. I am not gonna let you go no more! Not ever!'

Without thinking, Rose helped the girl to her feet and drew her up close. 'No,' she assured. 'Not ever. Come on.'

They ate at Pele's feet. Cold barbecued ribs, little squares of Bonito, a papaya to be shared between them, and a drink of cold clear lake water, scooped up in their hands. And then they settled back, hugging each other.

'We'll wait until dawn,' Rose instructed. 'Cuddle up now and let's get some sleep.' The tiny blonde head nuzzled into her again, and the older woman did her best to recall some of the crazy little stories that her half-French mother had spun out for her in those long-ago days in Baton Rouge. Eventually Josie fell asleep.

It was too cold for Rose to do likewise, and she had too much on her mind. Besides, she had already slept the afternoon away. She sat up with her back against the *maere,* the child's head in her lap, and watched the stars over her head. Now then, she told herself. You've made the child a promise. Now what? She had no answer. No matter which way her thoughts ran, she always came up against the rock that was Giles Gendron. The man she hated. There was no answer to be had. Gradually she let her thoughts dissolve away into shreds, leaving her mind a complete blank.

That half-daze, half-sleep was suddenly disturbed. The Coleman lantern, faithful to the moment, rattled, hissed, blinked, and went out. Instantly Rose snapped to attention. The night noises seemed to be amplified. She could feel eyes watching from out of the darkness, feet rustling in the undergrowth. Be calm, she told herself. For the child's sake, be calm! 'Yeah, sure,' she muttered. 'Be calm. I'm scared half to death and you want me to be calm! If I want to scream I will. Just shut up!'

She lay Josie's head down carefully in the sand, stripping off her blouse to stuff it under the child as a pillow. The wind coursing over her bare breasts reminded her how cold a tropical night could be. She fumbled around in the dark, bumped into Pele's *tiki*, and found the lantern. A quick shake verified her fears. There was no fuel left in it.

Damn, she muttered under her breath. I've got to have—a fire! Of course, a fire. She scrabbled around on the ground. There were twigs, tiny pieces of long-dead bark, and a little farther away, a pile of sticks. It was the work of a moment to pile them all up against the foot of the *maere*. The matches eluded her tired fingers. It took a triple effort to steady her hands, scratch the match, and plunge the flame into the wood. Six matches later she was rewarded with a tiny blaze, a mere speck of flame. She settled back on her heels near it, trying to convince herself that she felt the heat. The flame grew a little larger. She turned to Josie, moving the tiny body closer to the fire.

Her fingers were shaking. Her whole body was

shaking, in the grip of a massive fear. I'm a city girl, she told herself. It will all turn out okay. It will! It has to! Now that I know, it has to. While she was rearranging Josie's sleeping form, her back to the fire, she heard the noise. Louder than the other night-noises. A thud, a sliding step on pebbly sand. She froze in position, too frightened to turn around, too petrified to make a sound. Frozen. She stuffed a hand into her mouth to stifle her screams. If it doesn't hear me, she told herself fiercely, it won't notice me. It must be a bear. There aren't any bears in the islands. They're——

'Rose!' The deep voice behind her was laden with relief, almost as if he had feared more than he saw. Her muscles relaxed, and the scream came out, welling deep into the crater, rebounding from the soft darkness of the lake, echoing from the sides of the old volcanic peak. And then she collapsed.

After that moment when he had seen the light on Pele's mountain, he had wasted not a moment. As a result, he broke into the clearing barely an hour behind her, and went directly to the rocky ledge. This *has* to be the place, he told himself. A shadow moved, off to his right. He swung around, both hands up. A face moved into the light of his lantern. The *tahu'a*!

'She has gone to Pele's temple,' the old man said. 'I came too late to stop her. And the little girl?'

'I don't know,' Giles sighed. 'We haven't found her. Rose knows something. I don't know what. She's— Josie *has* to be up here someplace. Where?'

The old man stepped forward fully into the light. He was wearing his formal cloak of bird feathers, and carried what looked to be a war club in his hand. He pointed up the mountain. They plunged into the darkness, toe to heel. The weight of the first aid kit swung heavily against his hip as he moved, trying to keep up to the old man. We've got to hurry, he kept telling himself as he drove his legs harder. We've got to

find Rose! And Josie! Why in God's name did I put
Rose first? That niggling worry in the back of his mind
was still there. Why Rose? Why? She's only passing
through. She's going to Tahiti as soon as we find the
child. To go to her father's wedding. Hah! What a
sharp old man that one is. And Rose? Like father, like
daughter? Josie thinks the world revolves around her.
That's why I've been so patient with the woman. For
Josie's sake.

Like hell you have, his mind roared at him. Patient?
If you had been patient, things might be a lot different
right now. Remember what Rose called you? An arrogant
man! And it's true. Don't kid yourself that you've
chased all the way up this crazy mountain just for Josie!

The thought was like a slap in the face. He stopped in
mid-stride, astonished. 'But she hates me,' he whispered.
The solid darkness that was the *tahu'a*, ahead of him,
disappeared around a corner. He hurried forward to
catch up. The old man stopped suddenly, and Giles
almost ran into him. Directly in front of them, under the
lip of the cave roof, a tiny fire flickered, and behind it——

He ran the last few yards. Ran as if the devil were
behind him. 'Rose!' he shouted. The tiny woman in
front of him half-turned, screamed in wild fear, and
started to collapse. He was at her side before she hit the
ground, sweeping her up in his arms, treasuring her for
what he knew was her full value—all his life and love
and passion. 'Rose,' he whispered. 'I love you.'

One of her eyelids flickered. The eye slowly opened.
And then the other. Eyes filled with astonishment and
mad longing. 'What?' she croaked.

'Rose,' he repeated more loudly, 'I love you. I didn't
know it until just this minute, but I love you. You have
to marry me!'

She struggled up in his arms, sliding her hands
around his neck, feeling the warmth of his broad chest
flattening her breasts. Her shivering stopped. Of course

she told herself, what else could it be! She took a deep breath and kissed the tip of his chin. 'I'm glad, Giles,' she sighed. 'I don't hate you at all. I never did. I love you very much. And Josie too.'

An hour later her cuts and bruises had been seen to. The old man had brought the fire to a real blaze, and was now sitting with his back to them, cradling Josie's head on his lap. Rose curled herself up in Giles' lap and sighed a long thankful sigh. His arms were like a mighty bulwark, shutting out all the terrors of the night. And solving all my problems, she told herself fiercely. There was a warm glow permeating her being. Not fire-warmth, but rather man-warmth. Something she had heard about, but had never known before.

'You will marry?' the *tahu'a* asked.

'Yes,' Rose said dreamily.

'Wonderful,' Giles commented. His hand had been moving gently up and down her side, and now had come to rest just close enough to accept the weight of her generous breast. She could feel herself trembling again. Not shivering, trembling. He made concerned noises, not knowing the difference.

'Giles,' she offered hesitantly, 'I'm pregnant.'

'Wonderful,' he returned. His teeth nipped at her closest ear.

'It will be a wonderful little boy,' she dreamed out loud, 'and look like you.'

'Wonderful,' he repeated. He set her carefully aside, and began to struggle with the buttons on his shirt.

'Not possible,' the old *tahu'a* chuckled. 'Pele sends a girl.'

'Wonderful,' Giles contributed. He was trying vainly to stuff her into his shirt, but his wandering hands, reaching for buttons, sent explosions up and down her spine. Violent explosions!

'In that case,' she maintained primly, 'we'll just have to try again.'

A gust of wind swept across them. Inside his huge shirt she began to feel warm again. 'Don't forget,' the old man cautioned, 'when you leave the island you take Pele too.'

'Oh come on,' Giles snorted. 'That old superstition again?' The *tiki* swayed forward and backward, and then nosedived off its *maere*, straight at Giles' knee. He barely managed to get out of the way.

The old man chuckled. 'Pele say don't wait too long. I go down to the village. You come.'

'Yes, wonderful,' Giles said softly. His hand was still struggling with the shirt buttons.

'Maybe tomorrow,' Rose called after the old man. 'Maybe the day after tomorrow?'

The *tahu'a* waved to them in the semi-darkness. He had set Josie's head down gently on his feathered cape. They heard his laughter as he left. '*Iorana oe*,' he called.

Josie gave a little giggle, shifted on to her side, and began to snore. Giles' fingers were still at the buttons, undoing what he had worked so hard to do. Rose cupped his hands with hers, treasuring them for a moment, and then started to help him.

CHAPTER ELEVEN

THEY were married on the beach in Te Tuahine. The little chapel had been decorated. 'But it isn't big enough for the children to come,' Miri explained. And so the broad beach. The Anglican priest was a tall well-built Polynesian from Bora Bora, he wore a skirt of *pareau* cloth, and a frock coat. Sam Apuka stood behind the wedding pair, giving them a running translation as the ancient ritual, set in the Polynesian language, ran over their heads. She could feel Miri nudge her. 'I will,' she managed to squeak out. *'Ea.'*

There were blessings, and bowings and prayers. And then, in liquid English, the priest said, 'And I now pronounce you man and wife.' He beamed down at them, towering above their kneeling forms, and gently touched each of them on the top of their heads. He smiled out at the audience, and in melodic Polynesian, began a homily.

The audience shifted from foot to foot. A moment later, from the back of the crowd, a deep bass voice began to sing. Here and there, throughout the crowd, other voices joined in a haunting island melody. The priest continued for a moment, swimming against the tide, then gave up. He held up both hands and in a booming baritone, joined in.

'What's that all about,' Giles whispered to Sam.

'He about to make speech,' Giles laughed. 'Nobody wants speech, so we have *Himine*. Songfest. They sing something called "Now is the time for loving!"'

There was a small reception on the beach, and then Rose and Josie dashed up to the Big House, changing from the colourful *muumuus* they had worn for the ceremony, into more European clothes, for the trip.

The big *pahi*, decorated from stem to stern with streamers, signs, flowers, and love, awaited them at the dock. There were tearful farewells. Twenty-two paddlers—all the young men of the island, swept them out into the ocean for the trip to Maupiti, and the airport.

Giles stood beside her in the stern as they waved goodbye. 'Sam and Miri will stay at the Big House until we come back,' Giles explained to her.

'But I don't understand why we can't stay,' she protested. 'It's our home, isn't it?'

'I've told you why not more than a dozen times,' he teased. 'I want you where there are doctors and hospitals. And school for Josie. My daughter can hardly speak English. There's a house on the outskirts of Portland, Oregon, not half a mile away from an important person.'

'My grandma?' Josie prompted.

'Yes, love, your grandmother. My mother.' He tapped Rose on the tip of her nose. 'Any argument, lady?'

'Would it do any good if I argued?' she asked primly. She knew the answer already. If she did object, he would change his plans. But she had no intention of objecting. Life was perfectly wonderful, just being Mrs Giles Gendron. Perfectly wonderful! Just to complete the circle, she pulled Josie into the embrace they were sharing. The crowd cheered, and their long voyage had begun.

They found seats in the old airplane at Maupiti, and collectively held their breath as it wobbled bravely into the air.

'I'm worried about the *tiki*,' she told him. She patted the little case at her feet. It was an old leather container—a case for a cornet or trumpet, long disused. The *tahu'a* had produced it on their final day on the island. The little *tiki* fitted into it exactly, as if it had been carved in anticipation of this particular case. When he snapped the lid shut the old man pulled out an ancient Japanese writing brush and inscribed a complicated figure on its lid.

'Don't worry,' Giles chuckled. 'Forget everything except the trip.'

'Don't do that,' she snapped at him, brushing his hand aside. 'I didn't realise you were some sort of satyr. It can lead only to—to frustration, darn you. Josie's watching! Besides, if the customs people see the *tiki* we're in a lot of trouble!'

'Forget it,' he repeated. 'It's only a superstition.' But by that time their wheels had touched down at Papeete, and the little aircraft wandered up to the passenger terminal just as if it had a right to be there.

Her father was waiting inside the terminal. Her father, his new wife, and an official from the Mairie, complete with sash of office. The older man was looking a trifle subdued, but he hugged and kissed with French enthusiasm. Rose and her new stepmother took each other's measure at a glance, and liked what they saw.

'He is a good bank president,' the former widow Marceau confided. 'Who knows better how to guard the money than a reformed thief, no?'

'We've only got forty minutes,' Giles prodded. Qantas was the only airline with three seats open, and that only as far as Hawaii.

They needed hardly half that time. The official, in machine-gun French, raced through the civil marriage ceremony that made the religious service legal, and they caught up to their luggage just as the little trumpet case came sliding down the table. The inspector, a combination of Polynesian, Chinese, and French scattered through his genes, went through Rose's suitcase with meticulous care before making his chalk mark. His compatriot nudged him and said something about the time of flight. He laughed back as his hand was extended towards the little case—and stopped in midair. He stepped back from the line, bumping into the adjacent inspector, his big forefinger pointed at the little box and the symbol on top of it. If it were possible, Rose giggled to herself, he would actually have turned white. He held up both hands, and refused to touch another thing. From behind him a pure Polynesian looked over his shoulder and said, '*Sacré bleu*! Please! Take your luggage and go quickly!' Giles obliged, whistling as he went.

'Smart Aleck,' she told him fiercely as he stuffed Pele's box in the overhead rack.

They stopped over in Hawaii for two slow lovely days, before a flight offered to Seattle. It was a bumpy ride, but they hardly noticed.

'Aren't you two gonna do nothin' but look at each other and sigh?' Josie complained.

'That's all,' her father admitted. 'You have to get used to it, baby!'

'Well, that's silly,' his daughter complained. 'If I didn't like you both so much I'd be mad. Even when we get to Grandma's house?'

'Even when,' Rose chided her. 'You don't mind staying at Grandma's for a few days while Daddy and I—er—get the house ready?'

'Nope, I don't mind. Grandma's got dogs and horses and pigs. You two will need glasses if you keep that up. It must be some eyestrain.'

'Read your book,' her father glared at her.

'Don't do that,' Rose told him, pushing his hand away. 'What do you think can be accomplished in a public airplane?'

'Ah, but we'll be home soon enough,' he leered. 'I want to keep you tuned up.'

'Well cut it out,' she chuckled. 'You know you can turn me on in a minute. Behave yourself!'

There was a two-hour stopover at Seattle. As in Hawaii, not a word was said about Pele, hiding in her little case. When they transferred to the local feeder line, Rose put the case at her feet. They flew south at five thousand feet, low enough to feel the air pockets as they skirted the fringe of the mountains. Josie fell asleep, and Giles was deep in a sports magazine he had picked up at the Seattle terminal.

Rose wiggled her hand free from his absent-minded clutch, and pulled the little case up into her lap. One of the snaps was bent. It took her a few minutes to open it, and lift the cover. The little faceless statue stared out at her, and seemed to be feeling its new environment, the new world all around it. It quivered slightly in its box, and the airplane took a wild diving swing away from its smooth flight path and readjusted to a new course. The air seemed bumpier than before. Rose stared out the window. The loudspeaker activated with a metallic click.

'This is your captain speaking,' the voice said. 'We have just made a course correction, at the direction of the Portland airways control, and will approach to the city from the far south. If you look out your windows to the north, you will see the reason for the change.'

Rose leaned over Josie's sleeping form and peered out the window There, in the middle distance, surrounded by snow covered hills, a massive mountain top was stirring. Puffs of steam burst high in the air, and then suddenly there was a massive roar, the airplane was buffeted, and a great hole appeared in the side of the mountain. Giles put down his magazine and leaned over her to look.

'My God,' he said. 'Mount St Helens. The darn volcano is erupting! There hasn't been anything like that around here since—since God knows when!'

Rose squeezed back in her chair to give him room, and then glanced down into her lap. Inside her little travelling case Pele, the goddess of volcanoes, the *tiki* with no face, was laughing. Shaking the Earth!

Her husband pulled back and followed her glance. There was a peculiar—an unbelieving look on his face. As fast as her muscles could be made to move, Rose slammed the cover shut, snapped the locks in place, and let the whole thing slide off her lap on to the floor.

'Oh Lord,' she muttered under her breath. Her husband's face was inches from hers. 'It's only a superstition,' he chuckled. 'You're not responsible for all that!'

She sighed and took a deep breath, wishing she could believe him, but knowing that he was very wrong! '*Iorana oe*,' he told her.

'For ever after?' she queried.

'For ever after,' he repeated, and his lips sealed out all the sights, all the sounds, all the people, and locked them together in their own private world.

Harlequin Presents

Coming Next Month

Available in April wherever paperback books are sold, or through Harlequin Reader Service:

In the U.S.
P.O. Box 1397
Buffalo, N.Y.
14240-1397

In Canada
P.O. Box 2800, Postal Sation A
5170 Yonge Street
Willowdale, Ontario M2N 6J3

No one Can Resist . . .

HARLEQUIN REGENCY ROMANCES

Regency romances take you back to a time when men fought for their ladies' honor and passions—a time when heroines had to choose between love and duty . . . with love always the winner!

Enjoy these three authentic novels of love and romance set in one of the most colorful periods of England's history.

Lady Alicia's Secret by Rachel Cosgrove Payes

She had to keep her true identity hidden—at least until she was convinced of his love!

Deception So Agreeable by Mary Butler

She reacted with outrage to his false proposal of marriage, then nearly regretted her decision.

The Country Gentleman by Dinah Dean

She refused to believe the rumors about him— certainly until they could be confirmed or denied!

Everyone Loves . . .

HARLEQUIN GOTHIC ROMANCES

A young woman lured to an isolated estate far from help and civilization . . . a man, lonely, tortured by a centuries' old commitment . . . and a sinister force threatening them both and their newfound love . . .

Read these three superb novels of romance and suspense . . . as timeless as love and as filled with the unexpected as tomorrow!

Return To Shadow Creek by Helen B. Hicks

She returned to the place of her birth—only to discover a sinister plot lurking in wait for her. . . .

Shadows Over Briarcliff by Marilyn Ross

Her visit vividly brought back the unhappy past—and with it an unknown evil presence. . . .

The Blue House by Dolores Holliday

She had no control over the evil forces that were driving her to the brink of madness. . . .

You're invited to accept 4 books and a surprise gift Free!

Acceptance Card

Mail to: **Harlequin Reader Service®**

In the U.S.
901 Fuhrmann Blvd.
P.O. Box 1394
Buffalo, N.Y. 14240-1394

In Canada
P.O. Box 2800, Postal Station A
5170 Yonge Street
Willowdale, Ontario M2N 6J3

YES! Please send me 4 free Harlequin Presents® novels and my free surprise gift. Then send me 8 brand new novels every month as they come off the presses. Bill me at the low price of $1.75 each ($1.95 in Canada) — an 11% saving off the retail price. There are no shipping, handling or other hidden costs. There is no minimum number of books I must purchase. I can always return a shipment and cancel at any time. Even if I never buy another book from Harlequin, the 4 free novels and the surprise gift are mine to keep forever.

108 BPP-BPGE

_____
Name   (PLEASE PRINT)

_____
Address   Apt. No.

_____
City   State/Prov.   Zip/Postal Code

This offer is limited to one order per household and not valid to present subscribers. Price is subject to change.   ACP-SUB-1R